ANOTHER OPENING, ANOTHER SHOWMANCE

Point Pleasant Holiday Series #6

SHANE K. MORTON

Copyright © 2020 by Shane K Morton

All Rights Reserved.

No part of this book may be reproduced in any form or by any electronic or mechanical means, including information storage and retrieval systems, without written permission from the author, except for the brief quotations in a book review.

Names, **characters**, businesses, places, events, and incidents are either the products of the author's imagination or used in a **fictitious** manner. Any resemblance to actual persons, living or dead, or actual events is purely coincidental.

Cover art © 2020 by Winterheart Design, winterheart.com

Dedications

Special Thank you to Leona Windwalker and Michelle Frost! Lex Valentine, as always, I love the cover! I dedicate this to my new fur baby, Bette Davis. Thank you for crawling up in my lap while I wrote. You made it more difficult, but the love was worth it!

ACT ONE

1

Sebastian

"Hey, Seb!" Laurence shouted as he sashayed up to me. He believes sidewalks are runways, and his job is to *werk* them for all they're worth. He does it fabulously. "Where you been, sis? I was about to send out a search party before you called."

"You are so damn dramatic." I rolled my eyes as I grinned at him. It felt good to know my friends had missed me.

"Pot meet kettle. Now spill the tea, please." He pulled out his chair and plopped down. I had called and asked him to meet me at my favorite bohemian coffee place here in the Village, The Big Cup. It was gaudy and tacky, and I adored coming here whenever I could find the time. Sadly, I had discovered myself with too much time on my hands, and that was a problem.

"I know… I'm a bad friend," I sighed, knowing it was true.

"And…"

"A total asshat?" I scrunched my face up. I had no idea

what he wanted me to say, but the stern look on his face was not taking any prisoners today.

"Bitch! You didn't come to my birthday party. I turned thirty, child, and I needed all the support I could get. You didn't even RSVP." He pulled his Louis Vuitton satchel off his shoulder and set it down on the small metal table before crossing his arms and glaring at me.

"Shit… Did I really. I… uh… I honestly didn't see it in my email." I grimaced. Damn… I wouldn't have missed that. Laurence was one of my favorite people here in NYC, and I wouldn't have survived my first year here without him. I owe him a lot. "I… I'm sorry, puss. I've not been myself ever since the play opened."

"Uh-huh…" He pursed his lips as he stared me down. A slow, wicked smirk appeared, and he winked at me. "Okay… You're forgiven. But I expect a fabulous present to make up for it. Now, what the hell's been going on? I thought the play got great reviews, so why did you go all Norma Desmondy on us?"

"It was… I was drained and just needed to stop dealing with the world for a bit. I mean… This was my first big break, and I was so happy that the reviewers had so many great things to say about the production and the writing, but then… Well, I kept waiting, you know? Crickets… I just directed an Off-Broadway play that is critically acclaimed, and it's like the entire industry forgot about it overnight." I sat back and pried my shoulders off of my ears. This was why I holed up in my apartment for the last month. It was childish, and voicing my feelings out loud felt like a big baby whine of privilege. At least I got the opportunity. Thousands of people in this town didn't.

"Seriously? It's been a month. Damn, girl… Your play is still running. Becca with the big boobs told me she saw it last week and it was fabulous." His voice sing-songed, trying to raise my spirits. His eyes, though… They told another story. 'Grow up,' they mocked as his long eyelashes batted at me, curious as to what I was holding back if anything. "Child? You need to stop taking everything so damn seriously. You're gonna stroke out before you're thirty-two if you sit around waiting for Broadway to point their money laden fingers at you. If you hide away in your house, I promise you, they will forget your ass. Get out there and make them remember that you just accomplished a major win in this godforsaken town. Stop being such a…" He pursed his lips.

"Say it…" I shook my head, knowing I deserved it. He was right. I knew he was right.

"I'm not gonna say it… You already know you're acting like a drama queen, so I don't need to call you one." He shrugged as the waitress walked over to us. We ordered, and she scooted quickly away to get our coffees.

"Now that you are back to the land of the living, are you gonna tell me what happened to you and Ezra? I know that something happened, because big pecs-chicken legs, DeAndre, said he saw him making out with some charity case at The Saint. Wanna talk about the real reason you've been incommunicado, bitch?" He pursed his lips, waiting for me to spill the tea about the dramatic end of my abridged relationship. Sadly, Laurence would be disappointed in the flavor. It was weak.

"That was really not it. Ezra and I weren't right for each other in any way except one, and we couldn't live our life naked in bed together, so we decided to be friends. Seriously, that was it. Ezra was way too preppy for me, and you know it. Jesus, Laurence, he's an investment banker, and if it's not about what stocks are trending, he is not good company." I laughed as the waitress brought us our coffees. I thanked her, and she patted me on the shoulder before going back to work.

"Well, that is true. Ezra was Upper East Side adorable until he opened his mouth. I never did really like him." Laurence picked up his orange cup and blew into the hot liquid. "He was incredibly uptight, and I'm surprised he wasn't like that in bed. Color me shocked."

I leaned back and smiled. "He was very talented." I raised my eyebrows. Laurence reached over and gently slapped my hand in admonishment.

"You filthy bitch! So what now? Do you want to join me for the summer on Fire Island this year? I rented the beach house again if you want to escape from the city." He offered. I spent last summer with him there, and it was wonderful and full of too many damn debaucheries. It was tempting.

"Let me think about it, okay? You know I would love to, and it would be amazing to get out of this damn city for a bit. We'll see." I shrugged as I took a large sip of lukewarm coffee.

We sat and chatted for about an hour. He told me about all the gossip I had missed out on, and it was fun catching up. But something he said to me resounded deeply within me. I had been hiding away like I had failed in my most significant endeavor to date, which was quite contrary to the truth. I needed to strike while the iron was hot. I called my agent as soon as I got home.

Was it a good sign he immediately picked up?

"Sebastian, darling! Did you get the flowers? Were they lovely? They were supposed to be lovely and massive," he prattled quickly in his rapid-fire, no-nonsense way. I walked over to the small bar cart I kept in the corner of my living room. This conversation might require some liquid courage.

"I did, Jerry. Thank you, they were as gaudy as you wanted, I promise." I cooed, trying my best to appear happy and lighthearted. Calling my agent always made me nervous. For the last couple of years, every time the phone rang, I was afraid he was dropping me. Perhaps, now, I could relax about that. I did have a hit under my belt.

"Great! You never know… The cheap bastards. You pay for a forest, and they give you weeds! I hate those modern pieces of shit they call an arrangement! Always makes me sneeze. I was going to give you a call soon, my boy. Your play was a big enough hit that I've been sending your resume out to everyone, and I've had a few bites, so far. Nothing in New York yet, but there are some outstanding opportunities here, Seb. Most of these won't start pre-production and casting until late fall, so if I was you, I might take a vacation now, if you know what I mean." He talked so fast I had trouble following him. Did I have another job or not?

"So, do I have another job?" I asked. I poured myself a gin and added a dash of tonic.

"Not yet, Seb… These things… They take time, you know… But I think an offer will be coming this week for a great opportunity in Chicago and I think if it's offered, we should jump at it. It's a new show that has its eye on Broadway, and the investors are the real deal, so it has a great chance. Why do anything else when you can work with the movers and shakers that make shit happen if you know what I mean? Hang tight, Seb. I'll call you with news soon, I promise." He hung up. Jerry wasn't one for the standard niceties of hello and goodbye, so it didn't bother me, even if I was still as confused as ever. He was doing his job, and if he was right, this might be my last opportunity for a vacation for a while. I started to call Laurence, to agree on the Fire Island trip when my phone buzzed in my hand.

Shit. It was my Aunt Helen. I loved her, almost more than anyone else in the entire world. She's the reason I have a love for theatre and went into this fucked up profession. But I wanted to tell Laurence before the asshole invited someone else. He was like that. There would be ten of us living for the summer in a five-bedroom beach house. He had too many friends.

I hit ignore on my phone and was about to hit Laurence's contact when Aunt Helen called again.

Fuck.

Someone might have died. I was fatalistic, so of course, this was my first thought. I answered.

"Helen? Is everything alright?" I asked breathlessly, waiting to hear who had passed away. It was probably my Aunt Jillian. She was a wild child.

"Well… That depends on your definition, darling. I'm not dead, but sadly out of commission, and I need your help." Her firm voice made my back straighten.

"What do you need?" I asked, knowing that whatever she needed, I would be there for her.

"I fell, honey, and there's no way I'm going to be able to function this summer. I was only on the second step of the ladder, and I have no idea what happened. I guess my foot just slipped, and before I knew it, I was on the floor and in the most excruciating pain I've ever experienced, and that counts childbirth." She hissed. "Fuck, that really hurts. Are you gonna give me something else for this? Yes? Morphine… Morphine sounds lovely." I heard a muffled voice, I assumed a nurse answering her. "Sorry, honey."

"Helen, when did this happen?" I asked nervously.

"Yesterday. I have surgery this afternoon, and I can't

fucking wait. It's fractured, and they have to put some pins in." I heard her inhale sharply.

"What did you break?" I asked, wishing he would just give me the fucking facts. I was about as confused and nervous as I had been on my opening night.

"Oh, my hip... So, can you do it, or help me find someone, Seb? I know your show is still running, but I have to have someone to handle the summer repertory season. You think you might be able to find someone to help, honey? I need them here like yesterday." Her voice broke, and I knew what I was going to do. My summer plans were about to change.

"I can do it, Helen. Getting out of the city sounds lovely, and my agent doesn't have me anything lined up until the fall, anyway." I sighed. The Point Pleasant Playhouse was the stage I cut my professional teeth on. Going back there to work was going to be relaxing, and I did need to unwind.

"You have no idea how happy that makes me, Seb. How soon can you be in The Pleasant?"

This summer was not turning out the way I expected, but being in Point Pleasant wasn't the worst idea. Some of my best memories happened in that town. I called the airline and found a flight that would get me there with a transfer tomorrow morning.

I had to pack and quickly. What does one wear for a summer they hadn't planned for?

2

Sebastian

The flight got me into Dallas by eight in the morning. But the trip to The Pleasant was anything but quick. I waited for two hours until I could board the small plane that would get me across the vast lake from my destination. There I took the helicopter over the lake and into town. It was as jarring and exhilarating as I remembered.

When we touched down, right on the edge of town, I waved at the pilot and grabbed my duffel bag out of the small cargo net above. I hadn't brought much, so the bag was light. I had almost forgotten my swimming trunks when I was packing and remembered them at the last minute before I caught my taxi to the airport in NYC. I would be glad to have them. The lake and mountains were still breathtaking. The water was blue and clear, and the mountains still had snow at their tops, as they would all year long.

The Pleasant was a small village, but I knew its size was misleading. During the summer, it was packed with tourists. Some stayed for the whole summer, and others were weeklong or weekend visitors, and the playhouse would be jammed with them all summer long. It was a major tourist attraction in the town during the summer. The PPP, as residents called it, produced a three-show season every summer with professional actors from all across the country. I had directed my first professional show here, and before that had acted in various productions in my youth.

I wasn't from here, not really. My family was from Wisconsin, but my Aunt Helen had moved here many years ago and started the playhouse when she was in her early thirties. It had grown a lot since those first years. She had shown me many pictures of its evolution, and what she had accomplished here was amazing for both the town and herself. When my parents told her that I was following in her footsteps, she was elated to have someone to share her love of theatre with. I started spending my summers here in The Pleasant with her and helping out with all of the shows. It had brought us very close. Helen was my best friend as well as my family.

Hearing about her accident had broken something loose inside me. I hadn't been the best nephew in the last few years. I had become so self-involved as I worked to further my career in NYC. I should have called her more often. I should have made sure she was taking care of herself. Helen had never gotten married or had children. She was here in The Pleasant alone, and I knew, without a shadow of a doubt, even if I had been in rehearsals for a show, I would have dropped everything to come here. Love and family were always more important than a career. I needed to remember that when I returned to my life at the end of August.

I walked towards the middle of town. It hadn't changed in all these years, not really. Some of the businesses had altered, but the buildings were just as I remembered them. I had my first kiss with some townie boy, many years ago, here on this corner by the old ice cream shop. He had tasted of strawberries, and I didn't even remember his name.

The hospital was about a twenty-minute walk, but the air was clean and fresh, and there was a cool breeze coming from across the lake. It was a gorgeous day, and I knew, even when it did get warmer, it would still feel mostly the same. New York City was a beast in the summer. The oppressing heat and humidity and the stench of the garbage in that heat made the city a fucking sty in the summers. Point Pleasant was a sweet escape, even if I would be working most of the time.

I loved the beach here. For a lake, the water was crystal clear, and during the summer, it was where all the action happened. I would sneak off and lay in the sand, or play volleyball with a group of teenagers before we would all cool off in the pristine waters. Memories flooded through me and made me feel warm and cozy. I wondered what had happened to those teenagers I had become friends with? I had seen a few of them the summer after my freshman year of college when I came here to work at The PPP as an assistant director. Of course, my time wasn't as free then, so instead of seeing them on the beach, it was quick evenings as we drank beer at a bonfire. But our friendships didn't last. I was just someone passing through, and they lived here.

I found the hospital and went inside. A nice woman in a pink jacket gave me Helen's room number, and I walked down the middle hallway and peeked my head into room B24. She was sitting up in her bed, the remote in her hand, as she flicked between channels. Helen hated TV. It rotted your brain.

I knocked on the door-frame. She beamed at me and then grimaced as she adjusted herself.

"Helen? How are you feeling?" I walked over to her bed and took her outstretched hand. She squeezed gently.

"Seb, honey! Oh my god, you have no idea how happy I am to see you. Was your trip in, okay?" she narrowed her eyes at me.

"It was fine. So? How did your surgery go? When can you get out of here?" I asked, wishing I could have been here for her.

"Oh, it's fine. The doctor said I have to walk twice a day, even if it fucking hurts. It does… But I should be back on my feet by the end of the summer." She sighed and smiled again at me. "I am so glad to see you, honey. Thank you."

"Of course. I would have come even if you didn't need my help, you know that." I let go of her hand and pulled the small wooden chair near her bed.

"What time is it?" she asked suddenly. "Even one day in this damn place, and I've lost track."

"It's almost one," I replied, hating to watch the fiery diva I've always admired in pain.

"Shit. You need to go straight to the theatre. Oliver will be there by now, and he'll be waiting for you. Do you remember him?" Her hopeful face fell as she saw the confusion in my eyes. "It doesn't matter, honey. That was probably six or seven years ago now. You were both here for that disastrous production of Oliver, remember? He was my assistant for the summer."

I nodded. I remembered him. "Seven years ago. Glasses and messy hair?" He used to drive me insane. He was always around, and because he was from town, he knew all my friends even if he wasn't a part of their gang.

"Yep!" She laughed and winced. "Shit... Yeah, that is him. He is now on staff and is the technical director and designer at the playhouse. He's been a yearly employee since he came back from college. He will have to catch you up on everything. The shows are cast, and all you have to do is deal with the productions. Sandra is going to come and help you run everything else. She'll handle the box office and concessions and any office work that needs attending too."

"Am I supposed to remember her?" I asked sheepishly. My memories of the people I met here were jumbled up with all the coming and going I did.

"You used to play with her son, Evan. He was about your age, maybe a little older, lord, I don't know. She's had the same hairstyle since birth. Dark hair with bleached blonde streaks, and she has that deep laugh that sounds as if she's gonna blow out a lung. Does that ring a bell?"

I laughed. It did. I remembered her because of that hair. It was striking. "Evan! That was one of their names. I was trying to remember the people I used to know here, but I couldn't remember any of them. All I could remember is the super hunky guy was a lifeguard, and we used to stay on the beach a lot because of him."

"Danny. He's still a lifeguard, actually and is dating a movie star. You have a lot to catch up with, but after you settle in, okay? Now, I need you to go to the theatre and get caught up. Oliver, remember? He's great, and I'm sure you two are gonna get along. Now scoot."

I stood up and pushed the chair back.

"Oh, and Seb?" I turned back to her and noticed her eyes were misty. "Thank you, honey. I'm glad you're back... Even if it is because of this. Did you bring your key?" I nodded. "Good. Your room is just as you left it, sadly. There are fresh linens in the cabinet, and if you need anything, just call me, okay?"

"How long are they making you stay here?" I stared at her, scared of how hard it was going to be to keep everything up in the air at the theatre and to take care of her.

"A couple days. But don't worry about me. I have a friend that's coming to stay over while I heal, so you can focus on the shows. I… I don't want to be a burden to you, honey…"

I walked over and kissed her on her forehead.

"You are never a burden, Helen. I can help take care of you." I brushed her hair back out of her eyes.

"You sweet man. What did I do to deserve someone like you? Oh! Call your mother, please. She's probably worried to death." She smirked. It was a running joke between us. My mother was very high maintenance. "She called yesterday, and I told her you were coming. She wasn't happy that you didn't tell her. Call your, Mom, please."

"Okay, Helen. Theatre in the same place?" I teased.

"Get out of here. And Seb? I love you, honey." She pursed her lips together tightly. She looked older and frailer. Helen had to be in her late fifties, but she had always acted like a teenager. Her energy level was inspiring, and I did my very best to be like her. She was my rock.

"Love you more…" I answered as I grabbed my bag and headed to the door. "You want me to come back and have dinner with you?"

"Oh, God, no. Enjoy yourself, honey. I'll be home in a few days. I hate the thought of you having to be in here with me. Hospitals fucking suuuuuck." She grimaced again as she held in her laugh.

"Okay… I'll call you later," I said as I walked out of the room. I turned back and blew her another kiss, she reached up and grabbed it and held it to her heart.

The waterworks started as soon as I walked out of the

hospital. Seeing her like that was a shock. She had gotten older, and when something like this happens to someone, it makes them age even more. Helen… I really needed to relish this time as much as I could with her. Seeing her in pain… It was not something I looked forward to, and I felt terrible about that.

I crossed the street and headed towards the shore of Lake Pleasant. The theatre's bright awnings and large marquee greeted me as I turned the corner and spotted them a couple blocks away. The wind had picked up a little, and I could feel my hair blowing all over the place. I had forgotten that these streets were small wind tunnels when it was blowing like this.

I quickened my pace and moved over to the other side of the road. The beautiful green park I had remembered was a nice respite from the small open businesses that sat across the street. I noticed a coffee place and held out hope that fresh coffee would be waiting for me in the theatre. The cup I grabbed at the airport had worn off, and I was about to have a long day.

I opened the door to the lobby and walked inside. It hadn't changed very much. The bar had been renovated, and there were a few plush benches against the far walls. I walked across the tiled floor and opened the office door. No one was inside, but did my sense deceive me or was that the smell of freshly brewed coffee wafting across the musty office. I sat my bag down and walked to the back where a small kitchenette with a microwave and coffee maker sat on the formica counters. This hadn't been renovated since this place was built. It was kind of dirty. I made a mental note to clean this as soon as I could find some time.

I grabbed a cup off of the mug stand and poured myself a large cup of steaming coffee. Maybe Oliver knew

I was going to need this, or perhaps he made it for himself. Whatever… Finders-keepers.

The doors were open, so someone had to be here. Helen said Oliver was the tech director, so maybe he was in his own office or on stage. I walked back into the lobby and made my way into the auditorium. The PPP seated two-hundred and fifty patrons. For a small regional theatre, that was pretty big. This place was always filled with an audience. Of course, shows only ran Thursday thru Sunday, because the town had higher numbers of tourists on the weekends.

I saw Oliver on stage. He was bent down on all fours and looked like he was using his tape measure. Yeah… I remembered him. His hair was always out of place. I snorted as I took a sip and felt the burn in my throat. Cowlicks… He was always messing with his hair because it stuck up everywhere because of cowlicks. It was funny back then… He was shy and self-effacing, but I knew, even then, that he cared more than he let on about how people viewed him. He always tried to be perfect and made him a little high maintenance and hard to be around. Hopefully, he had changed.

He stood up and stretched. Well… He had definitely changed. He was broader and taller than I remembered. His muscular shoulders and back were not going to be a bad summer distraction.

I cleared my throat, and he turned around.

"Sebastian, is that you?" He covered his eyes with his hand and squinted out into the darkness where I stood. Stage lights were a bitch.

"Hi, Oliver. I hope you don't mind, but I stole a cup of coffee. Thank you." I strolled down the center aisle and admired the new crimson red upholstery that adorned the theatre seats. Helen had been busy.

"I thought you might need a pick me up. It's a long trip from New York. How's Helen doing?" He jumped down off the stage and walked up the aisle to meet me. I stopped and waited for him.

"She's doing fine. Cussing like a sailor," I answered. Damn... He had changed. Gone was the awkward and pimply face I remembered. Oliver had gotten handsome. His arms were covered in lean muscle, and the stubble he wore was quite entrancing.

"I'm sure. I was over there last night, and she called the nurse a fuckwit. They've been friends for years." He chuckled as he held out his hand to me. "I wasn't sure you'd remember me after all these years."

"I did. You've, uh... changed a lot." I murmured.

"Well, all the lifting and building here... You know." He flushed as he stuck his hands in his pockets. "I guess we better get started. Did Helen tell you anything?"

"She said the shows were cast, and you would catch me up to speed." I shrugged. "What shows are we doing?"

"Nunsense, Rent, and Noises Off. A breezy and fun summer season, as Helen would say." He grinned. Of course, his braces had come off too. Oliver wasn't really much of a looker back in the day, but he was fine as shit now.

"Nunsense is easy, but Rent and Noises Off are difficult shows to pull off with longer rehearsal periods. Do you already have designs completed?" I didn't mean to worry or sound like an asshole, but this wasn't going to be the easy season I assumed it would be. These shows were work.

"Oh, yeah," he grinned. "And I am really proud of how I have designed them this year. Instead of striking sets, we are building onto them. It will save us a ton of time and labor."

"That is smart. Noises Off is a bitch of a set, anyway.

A play within a play always sucks during rehearsals." He nodded. "Cool. Can I see them and maybe the cast list? When do rehearsals start, anyway?"

"Monday. So, in four days. We have a lot to catch you up on. Are you hungry? I've been laying out set pieces up there for a couple hours, and I'm starving. We could go over to The Pleasant Diner and get you a real coffee and a sandwich. Me too, of course." He brushed past me and headed towards the lobby. "Just let me grab all the folders. We can talk over there."

I followed behind. Oliver was a man with a plan, and as long as I could get more coffee, I didn't give a shit. What had I agreed to?

3

Asher

I usually waited all winter and spring for this time to arrive. This year I approached it with trepidation. I had been the musical director here at The PPP ever since I moved here. I love it, but this year was a wild card season. Helen fell off the damn ladder that all of us had told her to stop using. She acted like a young girl, but she was anything but, and this last year had been harder on her than usual. Getting older sucked. I had just turned thirty myself. I felt about eighty right now.

The PPP produces shows throughout the year except for January and February. It is just too damn cold. I loved The Pleasant, but the winters here were harsh. I had moved here when I was twenty-six. I applied for the musical director position the moment I saw it in Backstage magazine. I had needed a change. I was born and raised in Florida and went to college in Miami. After I graduated, I stayed in town and got a job at a gay karaoke bar. I started doing drugs, drinking way too much, and having sex with anyone who would provide me with the aforementioned substances. I realized after waking up in a pile of my own vomit that I had stopped being someone I liked.

I got clean and started looking for a job that might take me away from my past. Helen took a big chance on me, but after many phone conversations, she offered me the job. That woman saved my life. I owed her everything, and she had quickly become one of my best friends. She had even introduced me to a nice older man, here in town, that I promptly fell in love with. Jon and I spent three of the best years of my life together, and then last month, without any warning, he told me that it was time for me to spread my wings and fly. He broke my heart. I still don't understand why.

I drove to the playhouse and parked in my usual parking spot. The actors had successfully made it in town and were staying at the housing Helen arranged for them every year. Nunsense was our first show, and we had four actresses from out of town and an actress from town, Amber McGinty. She had become a staple here over the last couple of years. I adored her.

I was supposed to meet Helen's nephew Sebastian today. He was apparently this wunderkind who had just directed his first play in New York. Helen spoke very highly of him. I was nervous. He might be a dick. I mean, he was from New York. I read the reviews about his play, and they were all glowing. I should feel lucky to work with him, but all I really felt was nervous. My stomach was a hot mess, and I hoped it didn't get loud during our meeting. That's not an excellent way to make a first impression.

I walked up to the theatre and almost ran into the door as it flew open. Oliver gasped as he noticed he got very close to breaking my face with the heavy door.

"Oh shit! Sorry, Asher." He huffed, his face red with emotion.

"What's wrong. Ollie? You okay?" I asked as he crossed his arms.

"Nothing... I just needed to get out of there for a moment before I said something I can't take back." He darted his eyes back to the theatre. "Sebastian wants to change part of my design plans for Rent. He wants it to be more stripped-down, and that will make my turnaround for Noises Off a real bitch."

"Sorry, Ollie. I really liked them," I said, now worried about my own meeting with Sebastian. My stomach rumbled, and Ollie pretended to not notice.

"Yeah... Me too... But here's the thing... After talking to him, I have to fucking agree with him. He's right, and now I have to look at it all again and streamline it. The bones will still be there for Noises Off, at least. He may be as big a brat as I remembered, but he's fucking smart. Fucking prick." Ollie ran his fingers over his thick disheveled hair. He was one of those people I adored but never felt like I knew him a hundred percent. He kept to himself most of the time, and I admired that, even if I did think he was lonely.

"So, he's an asshole?" I asked.

"No..." Ollie frowned. "Frustrating, yes. He's a lot like Helen, actually. It's funny how I can take it from her, but the moment he opens his mouth, I can't decide if I want to punch him or kiss him."

"Really?" My eyes bulged out of my head. That was the first semi-romantic thing I have ever heard come out of Ollie's mouth. He was the quietest and most celibate gay guy I had ever met.

"Well... I already knew him and... Just wait. You'll see for yourself." He shrugged as he walked away. Cryptic... Hmmm... The nerves took control, and I felt my stomach flip as if I were on a roller coaster.

The door opened again, and an incredibly handsome man poked his head out. He was movie star material, and the moment his blue eyes met mine, I had to hold back my gasp. He was breathtaking. Tall and lean with a chiseled jaw and dark brown hair buzzed close to his scalp. He looked me up and down, and the frown slowly replaced itself with a small smirk.

"Are you Asher?" His baritone voice was soft, but I could tell he knew how to sing. It was just something musicians knew as soon as they heard someone speak. He could sing.

"And you must be Sebastian…" I held out my hand, and he took it in his own, offering me a firm handshake. "Ollie looked like he was headed over to Margie's if that's who you're looking for."

He laughed and held the door open for me.

"It's fine. Come on in. You know, the last time I was in The Pleasant, our musical director was older than the building. I didn't know he retired." He walked towards the auditorium, and I followed him. "He used to scare the shit out of me."

"Yeah. I only met Milton one time. He moved to Arizona to be near his daughter. He was burned out and ready to fly the coop. I know he and Helen still talk. She went down to visit him a couple of years ago and said he had lost thirty pounds and played golf." He laughed. It was pretty fucking magical. "Did you watch the audition tapes?"

"Of course. It's a good group, I hope. More singers than actors though. But it's Nunsense, not Shakespeare." He jumped up onto the stage with a bound. I walked over to the stairs and ascended them, walking towards the table he was standing by. He waited for me to get there before he sat down.

"So, I created a schedule. This show has a ten-day rehearsal period and then a three-week run. The cast of Rent gets here for a fourteen-day rehearsal period and then runs for four weeks. Noises Off also has a two-week rehearsal period and a three-week run." He handed me a stapled document as I sat down across from him. "I've never directed three shows in rep before, so this is a trial by fire. It's doable, but it's gonna be a bitch. We have some cast crossing over between the shows, so that means it's gonna be easy to burn them out or blow their voices out rehearsing Rent. The entire cast of Nunsense is in Rent, and that will be a challenge. That music is fucking difficult, and I don't want Nunsense to suffer, so we'll have to be very careful during that time." He pointed to the front of the schedule. "Oh, music is color-coded blue. Let me know how that works out for you. It's a tight schedule with music rehearsal and choreography as well as staging, but I think it works. You have any thoughts?"

I took a deep breath. It looked fine, and I agreed this was going to be a challenge. But Sebastian was a lot. Very direct and serious. It was hot... Usually, Helen and I make the schedule together a few days before rehearsals begin. Sebastian was type-A. He was in charge.

"This looks fine. Scores have already been sent to everyone, so they are supposed to come fairly prepared..."

"But we know how that goes, don't we? They'll come decently prepared but still in need of being whipped into shape. These actors mainly come from Denver and Los Angeles, right? The stage is not their forte. It's fine, I know that's what Helen usually does. I mean, New York is so far away, the cost would double for flights, but the quality of the actors would be so much better. Now, I have a question about Noises Off. Blake Hudson? How the hell did Helen get him to agree to do this?" He looked at me, dumbfounded. "He's a big star…"

"He lives here now. He and Danny Kinkaid started dating last fall, and he and Helen met for dinner one night. Apparently, he has always wanted to do this play." I noticed at the mention of Danny, his eyes widened.

"Danny… Yes! That was the name of the lifeguard. Helen did tell me about him dating a celebrity. Okay, now it all makes sense. Well, that's great for the theatre. Have you ever met him?" He asked seriously. "You think he's gonna be easy to work with or is he… You know, a celebrity."

"No, Blake is cool. I don't really know him that well, but I've seen him out and about, and he's always really down to Earth. I think you two will get along great. So, you know Danny?" I asked. Everyone knew Danny. He was so gorgeous he made Blake look like the guy next door.

"I used to spend my summers here, and I used to hang out with a lot of the kids from town. I just couldn't remember their names." He shrugged as if it didn't matter. "Great! I am glad the schedule looks good for you. I know that Helen and Oliver had the band behind the set for Nunsense, but I want to have them on stage. Since we need a two-story set for the other productions, I thought it would be fun to have the band up on the second story for Nunsense. I mean they are putting on a show, right? You think that will cause any sound issues in the theatre? Oliver said, I should ask you." He groaned. Apparently, he and Oliver had gotten into a dustup before today.

"I don't think so. It should mix well. This place has great acoustics, so as long as the sound guy mixes the voices well, that shouldn't be a problem." I answered, staring at his lips. They were full and plump. Kissable. I bet he kissed really nicely.

He snapped his fingers, and I could feel the gas bubble rumbling through me. "Did I lose you?" He peered at me, concerned.

"I'm sorry... I was thinking," About kissing you. "What did you say?"

"I asked if you wanted to grab dinner tonight and talk through any of this. I have to meet the choreographer next, and then Oliver and I have to look at the redesign, but we are gonna be working long hours together every day..."

"Yes," I said, suddenly cutting him off.

"Great. You want to go to The Moosehead. I haven't had one of those burgers in years, and I have been thinking about it." He grinned. He had such straight and perfect teeth. Damn...

"Sure. What time? Do you need me to pick you up?" I asked, hopefully.

"No, it's fine. I have Helen's car. She said to say hello, by the way. Seven?"

"It's a date. I mean... I will meet you there," I shotgunned fingers at him. OH MY GOD! Just fucking kill me. What the hell has happened to me? I have no game at all.

He chuckled and smiled at me.

"Great, see you at seven." I got up and waved goodbye at him and hurried down the aisle. I crop dusted the theatre as I made my escape.

4

Oliver

Being around Sebastian again is making me crazy. Damn him, if he wasn't so talented or looked like a GQ model, perhaps I would put my foot down and tell him to go fuck himself. I could… If I wanted to.

I could…

No. I wouldn't.

That's my problem, I've never been able to not want to please him.

Bastard.

I don't know if he remembers or not, but I used to follow him around like a goddamned puppy dog that summer we both worked here. If he went outside, I found a reason to follow him. He was beautiful back then too. He barely paid me any attention, he only had eyes for Danny, back then. I couldn't really blame him there. That was the case for everyone after they met Danny. I used to hate Danny because of how Sebastian treated him. He laughed louder at Danny's jokes and always managed to sit beside him when we had bonfires on the beach.

Jealousy was not a pretty look for me. When Sebastian

left, I knew he would walk back into my life one day. I thought he would visit or something, but he never came back. Now, here he was, and he was even more beautiful and talented than he was before.

Life… was not… fair.

But none of this really mattered to me anymore, did it? I wasn't the same dorky kid struggling with my sexuality anymore. I was a man who had dealt with all of that shit and was finally happy, even if I was single.

It took me a long time to look in the mirror and not hate the person I saw, staring back at me. But I did it. I overcame the shame and anger I carried around with me all those years, feeling like the one gay guy on the planet that everyone felt sorry for.

I didn't date much. That's true. The guys I met here in The Pleasant were all nice, but there was always something holding me back. Relationships were messy, and I preferred my life simple and without complication, even if it meant I went to bed alone every night.

Shit… This was going to be a long three months.

Especially if he was going to be brilliant and keep me on my toes with the designs for each show. His ideas were better, even if it was a faster turnaround between shows for the backstage crew and me. The asshole was right, and that didn't make it any better. Hopefully, he was finally done with changes for the season.

I wasn't proud of how I acted. It was childish, and beneath me, I know this. But it had been, 'Change this, Oliver,' and 'Wouldn't it be better this way, Oliver,' to the point I just wanted to scream. At least I didn't do that. I did, however, throw a tantrum before storming out when he questioned the Rent design. I'm not sure if it was because he was right or I was wrong, but all I could see was red, and I knew I had to get out of there before I said something I couldn't take back.

Margie's was the perfect escape.

Well, actually, Crystal was the perfect escape. Not much had changed over the last few years with her gaggle of gays and me. We got along and every now, and then I would join them if they were at the bar when I was there, but we didn't make plans together or anything. We weren't best friends… I didn't really have any of those. I found that if I kept people at a polite distance, life was more comfortable that way.

I guess Helen was as close to a best friend as I had. Most of the staff at the theatre were pretty cool, and we saw each other socially on occasion. It was a life in the theatre. It's just the way it is.

Being a theatre person, I was used to becoming friends with people for a month at a time. We bonded during rehearsals, and by the end of the show, we all went our separate ways to do it all over again with a new group of people. It's the way theatre worked.

I walked into Margie's and was surprised there were so many people sitting and eating at the tables. It was busy as shit in here, and it was well after lunch. Crystal was behind the counter, making coffee and some new girl I had never seen before was taking pastries and finished drinks to the tables. I walked up and took a seat at the counter.

"Hey, Ollie," Crystal waved at me. "Give me a second, okay? I have to make this mocha latte for the douche over there." She nodded to some guy in a suit. He did look like a dick. "Apparently he's FBI or something. Like I give a shit."

"No problem, Crystal. I'll just grab a pastry and an ice tea when you have time. I'm not in a hurry. Making that asshole wait can be my revenge," I muttered, apparently loud enough for Crystal to hear me cause she smirked and looked up at me.

"Ollie? Are you seeing someone?" She asked quietly, leaning across the counter towards me. "You have to spill the tea, Ollie. This gossipy queen wants to know."

"No... I... Uh... It's not like that... I mean... It's the new director over at the playhouse. He pissed me off and..." I stuttered. It's not that I didn't trust Crystal exactly... No, that's exactly it. I did not want to be the topic of her gossip with the boys. I was sure they already felt sorry for me, and I hated that it fleeted through my mind whenever I was around them. It had been like that since high school.

"Oh, Yeah... I was so sorry to hear about Helen. Is she okay?" Crystal said as she put the milk under the steamer and turned it on. She raised her voice to be heard. "Fell off a ladder... Jesus!"

"Yeah... She's back home and doing okay. It's gonna be a long summer without her, though at The PPP." I sighed heavily.

Crystal glanced back up at me. "So, who's taking over for her?" She said off-handedly.

"Her... uh nephew.... Sebastian. You know..."

"OH MY GOD!" She got so excited she splashed hot milk all over the place. "Slim! Holy shit!" She looked at me and got really quiet before pouring the milk into the mug. She slid it down to her waitress to deliver to the FBI douche. Crystal wiped her hands and came and stood in front of me. "Oh... The asshole is Slim, huh? You forget my friend, I have a very long memory. Are you okay?" she asked earnestly. I glanced at the ground. "Are you okay, Ollie?" she repeated.

I had to pause before answering. I wasn't sure if I was about to burst into tears or brush my feelings away as usual. Usual worn out. I grinned at her. "Many years ago, Crystal. I'm not the same boy that pined away for him. You know that."

"I know that the past is not always… the past, Ollie. Sometimes it rears its ugly head and becomes our present all over again. I hated to see how much pain you were in back then. Slim never had any idea, and I didn't want to interfere, but I should have let you know that I was there for you. I've regretted that for a long time." She reached over and put her hand on top of mine. "You said ice tea?"

"Yes… Thank you, Crystal," I sniffed, pushing my emotions back down. I could feel them bubbling up and threatening to explode out of me. That meant a lot… That I was seen…

"Should we have a party for Slim, Ollie? I think we should, don't you? Get the gang back together. I know they would all like to see him, and I have a special surprise for everyone, anyway." She poured my tea into a tall glass loaded with ice and pulled a jelly pastry from the glass case.

"Sure. I think it's a good idea, even if it does make me want to break out in a cold sweat," I sighed.

"We've all wondered what happened to him over the years. I think it will be fun, and who knows, Ollie. Maybe he will see how wonderful you are too?"

I should have kept my mouth shut.

5

Sebastian

Rehearsals begin tomorrow, and I should have stayed home and rested. Tomorrow is an easy day for me, though. The cast will be going over the entire score, and at the end, we will have a read-through with music. It's one of my favorite things about the process. Watching their raw performance as we sit around a table together is my chance to see who and what I will be working with. How I will have to mold them into the performance, they will eventually give.

I love it.

I was surprised that Ollie asked me to do something with him tonight. A peace offering, he suggested. I couldn't resist. That strange boy who had followed me around had become a very handsome man. I was intrigued, and I felt bad. He took pride in his work, and I could see that. He really was quite talented.

"Where are you taking me?" I asked as we strolled through the park. This was much more romantic than I had assumed. He was leading me towards the beach and not towards a bar as I had expected.

I glanced down and had an urge to grab hold of his hand. I didn't, of course… But I thought about it.

"You'll see, city boy. It's a surprise," he teased. "It's a nice night, though, perfect, one could say."

"You are surprising me, Ollie. A walk on a moonlit beach was not what I was expecting, exactly." I turned to look at him, he had a wide shit-eating grin plastered onto his face. He should smile more often.

"I'm full of surprises." He laughed. We got to the edge of the park and crossed the street. He took my arm, and I felt an electric spark shoot through me. It caught me entirely off guard. I almost pulled my arm from his firm grip but then realized he was guiding me down into the dunes and towards the beach.

I smiled at him. The moon was bright and close to full. I could see the smirk on his face as he tried to not look at me. It was maddening. This Ollie was much more enjoyable to be around.

A bonfire burned about halfway towards the shore, the tide rolled gently and breached against the sand. It reminded me of those nights from many years ago. I wondered if those kids down there were having as much as I used to when I was there age.

Ollie was guiding me towards them. Perhaps he knew a few of them and wanted to say hi as we resumed our nighttime walk.

"Is that Slim! Holy shit!" A woman's voice broke the night's stillness, and a shiver ran down my spine. I hadn't heard that nickname in years.

"Surprise," Ollie said quietly.

"I can't believe you did this. Thank you, Ollie, that's' very sweet of you," I said as a woman ran up to me with wild red curls. Crystal… Her name popped into my head.

"Hi, everyone!" I called out as she stopped in front of me. "Oh my God, you're a woman." I laughed.

"Your damn right, I am. Now let's get a good look at you, Slim... Hmmm... We're gonna have to change that nickname. You've filled out. Hi Sebastian." She reached up and wrapped her arms around my neck and pulled me into a hug. I could feel Ollie let go of my arm. My skin grew cold and shivered, where his fingers had been.

"Hi, Crystal. It's really good to see you again," I said into her ear as her hair tickled my nose.

"I didn't think we ever would. You were a part of our summers for years, and then you just disappeared after your freshman year. We've always wondered what happened to you. Come on, everyone is excited to see you again." She took my hand and pulled me towards the roaring bonfire. "Don't worry, we now drink good beer instead of that shitty piss water we used to steal."

"Sounds great... God, I hope I remember everyone's name."

"Don't worry about it. They don't remember their own name either," she laughed. "Hey guys, he's here."

A tall, broad-shouldered man with dark curly hair jumped up and ran up to me. He grabbed me around the waist and lifted me up, spinning me around before setting me down. "Slim! It's been too long."

Danny had barely aged. He had only gotten even more fucking handsome. Of course, those looks helped him land a Hollywood star. My pulse beat rapidly, being this close to him again. "Danny! Jesus... You're breaking me in half."

He set me down and took a step back. A very familiar face walked up behind him, and I knew that this was Blake Hudson. His face was everywhere during the TV season. "Sebastian meet Blake. I guess you two are working together this summer."

Another Opening, Another Showmance

He held out his hand, and I shook it. He was just as handsome in person, and that smile was dazzling. He was going to be great in Noises Off, I hoped. "Sebastian, it's a pleasure to meet you. Your aunt has told me so much about you. Your reviews for your last play Off-Broadway were spectacular. We're lucky to have you here."

"Are you kidding me? I'm still a nobody, but having you here at the playhouse is good for everyone. I'm looking forward to it. Noise's Off is a great play," I enthused. Directing him was going to be good for my resume, even if it was here in a small-town playhouse.

"Alright, you two. Enough shop talk," Crystal grabbed my hand and pulled me towards a bench. Each of them stood up and hugged me. It was nice. Wally was just as loveable as ever, and Evan just as uptight. His husband Everett looked and acted so much like him it was almost comical, yet somehow sweet.

I almost didn't recognize Sam. He had really grown into a handsome man. Hunter looked exactly the same, and so did Kris. The last year I was here, Kris had moved away, and Hunter was devastated. Glad they got back together.

"So, what's been happening over the last... Jesus... Seven years? Is that right? Sitting here right now, it feels like last summer," Sam laughed.

"Hey! Where's your daddy?" Wally asked suddenly. It was a strange question...

"We couldn't find anyone to watch Lilly, so he sends his love." Sam saw the strange look on my face. "My boyfriend Claybourne is a little older than the rest of us."

"Sam has always appreciated a good father figure," Hunter laughed, and Sam joined him.

"Well, we are almost all here. I think there are a couple people missing, right. Where's the other ginger... Shit...

Dylan? And what about Tyler?" I laughed loudly. "Sorry, but I can't believe everyone's name has finally come back to me. I guess all I really needed was to be here to jog my memories. Tyler… Good grief. He gave me my first kiss."

"Mine too," Kris laughed.

"No, shit? He gave me mine too," Evan responded.

"Would you believe that he gave me my first kiss, also?" Hunter piped up a shocked look on his face.

"No," everyone said loudly, and we all started laughing.

"That was me," Danny said sheepishly.

Everyone looked over at him.

"What? We were in like eighth grade, and neither one of us had ever kissed a guy. Hunter had very soft lips," Danny threw a small punch and hit the incredibly muscular Hunter on his large bicep.

"Football bros," Hunter grinned.

"Yeah, we haven't seen Tyler in quite a while. He got into a little bit of trouble one night, and his parents sent him to military school. I heard he enlisted, but we've not heard from him since." Crystal said softly. "And Dylan is marrying a prince."

My jaw fell onto the sand, and my eyes bugged out of my head. Everyone nodded as if it weren't a big deal. I turned to Oliver, who smiled at me.

"Yep, a prince from Allyria. They're getting married this Christmas. It put Point Pleasant on the map for a while." Ollie nodded.

"Yes, darling. Between Liam, that's the prince, Blake, and Lucas Morgan, The Pleasant has been in a lot of magazines lately," Crystal stood up and clapped her hands. "I see my surprise is right on time. Gentlemen, if you will," She pointed her finger at Danny. "Danny Kincaid, don't you dare look over your shoulder. Your eyes, mother fuckers, better stay right here on me."

To her credit, no one looked around. Crystal had always been in charge of these boys, and I could see that nothing had changed. I glanced at Ollie, who was shaking his head, finding the whole thing funny. He had never been a real joiner…

"Okay, now that I have your attention. Tonight it is not only Sebastian 'Slim' Olivier who has returned to The Pleasant. We also have another visitor. Gentlemen, please stand up and prepare to offer your hand to his royal highness, Dylan Keller of Allyria." She said loudly, her cackle just as I had remembered it.

"Hi guys," Dylan said as he walked around to the front of us, a large smile on his handsome face.

Everyone walked over to him and hugged him, murmuring their hellos and love to the young man that I had remembered as painfully shy. Holy shit… He's marrying a prince. Of course, I had read about the American and the first gay prince, they were major headlines last Christmas, I just never made the connection to the young man I used to know. Point Pleasant was no longer the sleepy town I used to know, it had changed and grown, even if you couldn't see it with your eyes.

"I swear, I wanted to tell you I was coming in, but Crystal made me keep it a surprise." Dylan waved at me. "Hey, Slim. It's good to see you." I saw him gesture to someone behind us. We all glanced back and saw a man dressed in a black suit, standing with his arms crossed. He was massive.

"That's Peyton. He doesn't speak much. He's my… uh… bodyguard. The queen wouldn't let me travel home without him accompanying me." Dylan shrugged. "Just ignore him. That's what he prefers. It's no big deal."

"No big deal," Crystal blurted out. "Are you not going to tell…"

"No big deal, Crystal," Dylan blurted loudly, cutting her off. His eyes darted over to her and flashed a warning. It was obvious, and everyone felt it. Crystal crossed her arms and glared back at him. It was kind of tense. We all just stared at them until finally, Hunter broke the tension.

"Who wants another beer?" Hunter asked, sticking his tongue out at us. It was silly, and everyone chuckled. But we all still felt it. Something was going on, and Dylan did not want anyone to know.

We all sat back down and caught up. It really was a lovely evening. I could feel Oliver next to me, his presence made me feel safe. I was not really prepared for that.

After four beers and a couple hours of laughter, it was time to go. Danny and Hunter extinguished the fire, and we made plans to see each other again. Oliver and I walked back towards the theatre where we had left our cars.

"That was a real surprise, Oliver. Thank you. I was hoping to see a few of them again." I reached out and patted his shoulder gently. "I had some really great times with all of you."

"Yeah, I know," he shrugged as he kicked a stick out of our way. Little beads of sand flew into the path in front of us. "I never really felt like I belonged with them, you know. They were so much cooler than me and popular… I was… slower in figuring it all out than they were. It's always been hard for me to… make that connection… Let myself… Put myself out there."

"You've come a long way from that shy fellow, Oliver. You seem strong and sure of yourself now," I smiled at him, not wanting to interrupt his revelation, but to let him know that I saw him.

"Well… Sometimes, I… It's not any easier, Sebastian. Sometimes, especially when I am around those guys, I feel like I turn back into that bumbling kid again, sitting on the sidelines watching all of you live a life I dreamed about." He took my elbow and helped me walk up the steep path back to the street level.

"You sure did follow us around. We would have been cool with you being a part of the gang, you know." I said seriously.

"It wasn't them I was following. Not really," he said, looking away from me. "Besides, I saw them through the year and… Well, I'm not really a part of them, but I hang with them when I see them out every now and then."

"So, you were…"

"Here we are, Mr. director. I guess I will see you tomorrow," he said quickly, making an escape from the conversation.

I watched him get in his truck and start to pull away. He stopped and waited for me to get in mine.

Ollie was a conundrum. I thought about him all the way home and still wasn't sure what he was about to say.

6

Asher

The first couple of days during rehearsal, you can always tell me how the season is going to go. Nunsense was turning out to be a blast. All of the girls came in prepared, and we worked out the harmonies quite easily for the group numbers. We began learning the dances the next day, and Liza, our choreographer, put the girls through the paces. Sebastian watched from the back, every now and then, calling Liza or me to have a quick conversation about what he was seeing. He began staging the show today, and I have to say, as much as I love Helen, Sebastian is the real deal.

He was able to get through the first act pretty quickly. I sat in the back and watched as he brought the show to life. The actresses hung on every word, and as he gave them their blocking, he offered words of advice on the text. They loved him, it was obvious. He was easy on the eyes and had a vision for the show that everyone loved.

He called a quick break before we began the first walk-through of Act one. The cast would have a quick break after before they began choreography again with Liza.

Sebastian looked up at me and grinned as he gestured for me to come to the front of the stage. I walked down the center aisle and stood at the base of the stage. Sebastian sat down in front of me.

"Looking good so far, and they sound amazing, except for the patchy high A flat at the end of the first group number. Can you work with her on that, or maybe switch it to Amber. You were right, by the way, she is really fucking great. That voice… It's exceptional." He picked up his notepad and scanned down his list. "Besides that, vocally, I think they sound great. Good Job, Asher. You're quite easy to work with." He glanced over at Liza. "What's her deal? She's hard to get a read on if you know what I mean."

I leaned in. "Liza used to be a Rockette, and she hurt her achilles during a tour. Never really recovered from it, so she retired and moved here. I think it's her grandma that lived here, so she moved to be closer to her. I think she's had her studio here for the last four years. All the little kids take classes there, and she even does some older adult stretching classes for seniors. She stays to herself, though. She and Helen have formed a bond, but she doesn't really hang out much with the crew. Nice enough, though, just… She's a little aloof." I smirked.

"So she was in New York? Thanks, Asher… That will give us an actual ice-breaker. She's been all business, so far." He stood back up and turned to our stage manager. "We have what another ten?" Abigail, our stage manager, nodded. "Great. I'm gonna go grab some coffee. You want anything, Asher?"

"Nah, I'm fine. Thanks, Sebastian."

He walked over to the side of the stage and descended the stairs before disappearing out the side door. Sebastian was the kind of man you liked to watch walk anywhere.

"I think someone has a little crush," Amber said from behind me, her hands resting on my shoulder.

"No… I… uh… I was just…"

"Relax, Ash… I meant him. But you did seem to enjoy the view," she laughed easily, moving around me and leaning against the stage,

"Him? You think he? No…" I managed to get out, but the seed she planted started to root inside my brain.

"I'm just saying what I think I see, Ash. He glances over at you quite a bit." Amber grinned as she reached up and stroked my cheek. "I just want to see you happy, hon, and you haven't been ever since…"

"Jon made me feel like I was a disposable piece of shit. Yeah… Me too." I sighed. My neck muscles tightened and almost made me flinch in pain.

"Still hasn't told you why Ash? That really sucks and doesn't make any sense to me," Amber said sweetly. I had grown to appreciate her friendship over the last year.

"No. I think he told Helen, though. All she said to me was that he was an older man who was trying to work it all out and to give him time. It's been over three months now, and I can't keep waiting, can I?" I asked, hoping for a little guidance. Decisions have never been something I was very good at. It took me an hour to decide on what polo or sweater I was going to wear.

"It happened to my grandpa too. Be woke up one day and told my grandma he wanted a divorce. Found out, he had cancer and didn't want to put her through that. Of course, they didn't get divorced, and she gave him a piece of her mind. But maybe he was going through something and didn't want to drag you into it. I don't know, Ash. But I do know that you deserve to be happy, and Sebastian is beautiful and seems to be into you. So, I say go for it. Ask him out." She leaned in and gave me a hug.

"A date… You know I can't remember the last time I asked someone out on an actual date. In Florida, I was great at hooking up, but dating…" I grimaced.

"No time like the present. Just ask him to go out for a drink or something. I bet he says yes."

She grabbed her script and jumped up onto the stage. "Seize the day, Ash."

She left me standing there alone with my brain flooding with too many questions. Sebastian? Was he into me? Was I into him?

"Penny for your thoughts," Sandra said as she plopped down in a chair in the front row. I turned and smiled at her, she held up the cross-stitch she was working on.

"I think I would owe you change," I chuckled, shaking my head to clear out the thoughts still spinning through my mind.

"Oh honey, that's all most thoughts are worth. Me, I would rather be sitting at home doing my needlepoint and reading a good mystery. If Evan would just adopt me a grandchild, I might have something to look forward to," she huffed. "How are you and Seb getting along? I thought he had broken Oliver for a bit. He being nice to you?"

"Yeah, he's been great. He is everything that Helen said he was," I replied.

"He's grown into an incredibly handsome man. At least we can all enjoy the view." She darted her needle in and out of her small hoop. "Maybe I'll make him a little something to remember this summer by. According to Helen, his star is on the rise, and he will be too busy to mess with any of us again. I do wish him luck."

"Yeah… You are probably right. Sorry, Sandra, I have to check on what's next," I lied, making my escape. I wondered out into the lobby and sat down on the bench against the window. I could feel the sun's heat beaming in at me.

Sebastian was just passing through. Sandra was right. Even if he did have a little crush on me, something I still doubted, it didn't really matter, did it? He had his own life, and I had mine. Perhaps that was what was wrong with Jon and I. Maybe I cramped his style.

I had to stop feeling sorry for myself. I needed to brush the past off and look forward to something else, even if that something else was just a momentary distraction.

"You ready, Asher?" Sebastian's voice caught me off guard and made me jump.

I looked over at him and stared a hole into him. "Yeah," I shrugged. "Hey, Sebastian… You wanna go grab a drink later tonight?"

He looked down, and I was about to tell him it was ok if he didn't want to when he looked up at me and smiled.

"Sure. I can't see why not."

Even though he said yes… He made me feel a little sad.

7

Sebastian

What is happening?

I come to Point Pleasant to get away from my life, and suddenly there's a hot boy on every corner catching my eye.

Oliver… Now there is someone who has no idea what he wants. He is nothing but confusing. He keeps giving me all of these mixed signals that have made me head spin. One moment he is taking my arm, and the next, he just glares at me all day. We've barely spoken a word during this first week of rehearsal, so maybe none of it has meant anything, and I was reading way too much in his touches and kind words.

I spent days trying to figure him out. Finally, I decided my time was best spent worrying about the show instead of the hunky designer, even if he did look quite stunning in his tank top and tool belt.

As soon as I started to settle into my groove, along came Asher, which really was a surprise for me. He was so quiet and milquetoasty that I would have never thought of him in a romantic way, even if he was uber adorable. The perfectly coiffed blonde hair made me want to run my fingers through it and see what would happen if he let his guard down. He never seemed to let his guard down.

Asher and I have gone out for drinks almost every night this week, and it's been great. He's told me a little about his past, and it was quite surprising. He doesn't seem like the type of guy to have ever been a big partier. His stories caught me off guard. The man that sat across from me seemed to have it all together. The wild child he was in Florida made no sense to me as I stared into his eyes.

Of course, I noticed he only ever had one cocktail. He was hyper-aware of keeping his addictions at bay. He worked in a gay leather bar as a bartender. I was sure that meant he had some pretty skanky stories. That part, he kept private, sadly.

Even though we spent all this time together, he had yet to make the first move. He asked me out, and I was starting to wonder if I had misread his signals, too.

Dating in The Pleasant was not coming easily to me, and dating where I worked was usually a very big no-no for me. But the laid-back pace of everyday life here crept into me and made me relax my inhibitions. I was curious where they might lead.

"So, where do you want to go tonight? I thought we could go back to The Moosehead. I'm a little hungry." Asher blushed, which was fucking adorable on him. When he got excited or nervous, he flushed all over, and I noticed it was mainly around me. I started to answer but stopped when I heard a scoff from behind the lighting console. Oliver's eyes were boring into me, watching me as I talked to Asher.

I reached out and put my hand on Asher's shoulder, looking up at Oliver, daring him to say something. He turned the small lamp he used when he was working back there off. His face was now bathed in darkness.

"Sure. That sounds great. I wondered if you were gonna want to go and grab something tonight." I smiled at him sweetly.

The truth is, as cute as Asher was, he didn't really make my stomach do flip flops. He was nice and easy and completely unchallenging. If we were to have a difference of opinion, he would quickly sway to my side. There was no fire there, no combativeness to assert itself against my very well-formed thoughts. I craved that. I thrived on it. Asher, bless his heart, was not my type at all. Which was okay, in the long run. I mean, I wasn't looking for a boyfriend, was I? I would be leaving here in less than three months to go back to my own, hopefully, very busy and successful life. A long-distance boyfriend was not in my future.

Asher was convenient, and he made me feel good. Asher would be a very good friend with benefits. We were both, after all, directors here at the playhouse, so it wasn't like I was his boss. Not that I hadn't had trysts with actors before, because of course, I had.

"Let me go and get my bag, okay?" Asher asked, and I nodded. I didn't want someone to ask permission. I wanted them to tell me what they were doing. Shit… I should end this before it gets any messier, and he actually falls in love with me.

"Asher, huh? Didn't think that would be your type," Oliver's voice growled at me from the shadows. "Be careful, Mr. Broadway. He's a fragile boy."

I admit it. Oliver made me angry by even talking about it. He got under my skin, unlike anyone else I had ever met, and it drove me crazy.

"Seems all man to me," I said snidely. "At least he

knows what he wants and isn't afraid to go for it. He's very… nice."

"That he is…" He stood up and walked up to me until his face was mere inches from mine. I could feel his hot breath, and it smelled like coffee. "Just remember that before you go and break his heart."

He turned and walked away from me, leaving me standing alone in a furious stupor.

Fuck you, Oliver… I will show you exactly what I think of him.

Asher came back into the auditorium and brushed past Oliver at the doorway.

"Got it. You ready?" He smiled.

I walked up to him and took the backpack out of his hands and leaned in and kissed him gently.

Asher's hands wound their way through my hair, and he gently pushed his tongue into my mouth. It was… nice. I saw Oliver turn around and smirk at me, his eyes catching mine as I kissed this other man. He shook his head and disappeared. I gently pulled away from Asher.

"That was… Wow! Oliver, I've been trying to figure out how to do that for days." Asher blushed.

Nice…

Fuck.

8

Asher

I love openings! Everyone is so excited, and I mean everyone. The cast is thrilled to finally be in front of an audience, and our audience is always electrified to be the first to watch the show. It's like that with every opening night, but the summer shows at The PPP are even more fun than the normal community shows we produce the rest of the year. During the summer, the audience expects greatness, and this show has that *wow* factor people clamor for.

A large part of that is because of Sebastian. He has elevated all of our work and made us dig deeper than we normally do. It's been frustrating and thrilling all at the same time. Sebastian expects greatness. I think he got us to deliver at a level above what we normally do.

I am really proud of this show and cannot wait to start Rent next week. Just to be in the room with him as a colleague is enough. However, I have gotten a little more.

He is just so beautiful and fucking talented. It's not only inspiring. It's liberating.

I just wished…

Well, he is not Jon. That sucks, knowing that even if he did fall madly in love with me, I would still be thinking about the man who left instead of the one standing in front of me.

I mean, I have really loved the past week. It felt nice going out places with a beautiful man who gave me the attention I needed. My ego had been more than bruised lately, and Sebastian's glances and tender kisses have helped to heal me in some ways. He has made me think of myself as worthy, once again, and after Jon dumped me, I needed it.

I just wished I could have closure. Maybe I could move on if I knew why Jon let me go. Knowing wouldn't be half as bad as wondering what I did to make him quit loving me.

After all of this pain, I know I would still come if he called. What the fuck was wrong with me?

"It's a great crowd," Oliver startled me. I almost spilled my ice tea all over myself. I swear that man is like a ghost sometimes.

"Jesus, Oliver!" I hissed, making myself chuckle. "You scared the bejesus out of me."

He laughed. Oliver was one of my few friends here in The Pleasant. We weren't exactly close, I guess no one was really close to him. He was one of those people that everyone liked, but no one could say they were good friends. I don't know what happened to him when he was younger, but it made him a man of mystery.

"Sorry. I didn't mean to make you take a bath here in the lobby." He scowled. His dark eyes locking onto mine. "But this is a sold-out crowd, and that's a great sign for the summer. If Nunsense brings in this kind of audience, rent is going to be standing room only."

"We can only hope. Seriously, this show is pretty

fucking awesome, though. It's a great way to kick off the season. Your set design looks fantastic, Ollie." I grinned at him.

"Where's the boss man? Is he still in the back primping?" Oliver smirked. There really was a tension between him and Sebastian. Anyone could see that. It was unhealthy.

"I haven't seen him since the cast did their warmups. Maybe he went back to Helen's to change. Have you seen her yet?" I asked. "Sebastian said she was planning on coming. She even rented a wheelchair for it, he said."

"She's not here yet. But Sandra reserved her wheelchair space in the back, so I know she's supposed to be here." He looked at his watch and narrowed his eyes before glancing back at me. "Fifteen minutes before curtain. I'm gonna go talk to the ushers. They need to open the doors, or we're never gonna get everyone inside in time."

He took off and headed straight to the house manager, Henry, who had been here longer than any of us. I laughed because that conversation was not going to go well. No one messed with Henry. He was eighty years old and no longer gave a shit.

"I guess I will forgive you for not coming to visit me during rehearsals," I turned around quickly to see Helen rolling up to me. I started to grin at her but almost dropped my glass instead. Jon was the one pushing her, and he looked extremely uncomfortable at seeing me.

"Helen… Jon," I managed to say before my mouth zipped itself shut. I was in shock. I could feel my shoulders slide up to my ears, and my spine crack as it went rigid.

"Hello, Asher…" He said quietly. Helen slapped his hand from her chair.

"Jesus Christ! You two are the most frustrating human beings I have ever met, and that's saying something. Will you two, please go outside and talk, and I'm serious, Jon, you need to tell him. I'm sick of it. Why people choose to be miserable instead of happy is beyond me." She steamed as she stared at us. Her eyes glancing back and forth from me to the older burly man who looked like he was about to burst into tears.

It broke my heart, the look on his face…

"Oliver!" Helen shouted over my shoulder. "Honey, will you take me into the theatre?"

Oliver brushed past me and planted a quick kiss on her cheek. "Of course. Hi Jon…"

"Oliver," Jon nodded as he glanced over to me.

Helen pointed at Jon as she rolled away, Oliver behind her, guiding the wheelchair through the entering crowd.

I guess the house manager agreed with Oliver. Shocking.

I crossed my arms and stared at Jon. He looked like he was about to vomit. He always looked green around the gills whenever he got nervous. I could see the perspiration beginning to bead upon his brow.

"Can we talk?" he asked sheepishly, glancing away from me to stare at his shoes.

"Follow me," I nodded at him and scooted past a little old lady with a cane, so I could take us outside. I walked quickly through the open doors and moved over to the side of the building that faced the beach. The sound of the gulls flooding my ears as their calls echoed off of the brick exterior. I turned and saw him slowly following behind me as he passed and turned the corner.

"I… uh… How are you, Ash?" he said as he walked closer to me.

"Oh, I think you know how I am, Jon. It's been a pretty shitty year. And yourself?" Acid dripped from my tone. Was that the best he could muster?

"I deserve that, and I agree… It's been a real crap show these last three months. I'm sorry, Ash… I… Are you seeing anyone now?" He looked out to the open water, and his shoulders fell. One of the things I had always loved about Jon was his *joie de vivre*, his love of life, but that emotion seemed dulled and lost to the person standing here with me.

"I don't think that's any of your business, actually," I said slowly, letting my words cause the damage I wanted them to.

He glanced away from me again and raised his hand up to his face. It didn't make me feel any better. In fact, I felt worse. I thought I wanted to make him hurt as bad I did. But at that moment, I realized he already did.

"You're right…" he sniffed. His shoulders tensing as he tried to calm himself. "It would serve me right… You're young and beautiful and always have been too good for me…"

"Too good for… What the hell are you talking about, Jon? I'm a hot fucking mess, and without you, I've been so fucking lost… I just don't understand. I thought we were happy, and then… You just leave me like a piece of trash." I walked over to him and stood beside him, placing my hand tentatively on his shoulder. He turned around, and I could see the tears flowing down his face.

"I didn't want to… I mean, I knew it would hurt you… but, Ash… I'm too old for you. You deserve a chance to find someone to love who's closer to your age. I'm almost sixty years old… An old man and I'm only going to get older, and you are so young… "He hung his head and glanced quickly over at me.

"Is this why?"

He shook his head slowly, and I laughed loudly.

"Ah… Are you kidding me? This is because you are

turning sixty, isn't it? You doddering old fool... I don't care about that. I told you when we first started dating, that age meant nothing to me. I love you, Jon. I want to be there with you through all of it, don't you understand that?" I said softly, the anger falling away from me and replaced with pity. It wasn't me... It had never been me. It was his own insecurity about our age difference. He thought he wasn't good enough for me.

He turned to face me and took my hands in his. "I know... I... It... Yes... I thought about the fact that I'll be in my sixties this fall... And... It felt so old, Ash. I looked at you the night before, and I thought to myself... What am I doing to you? How I was stealing your youth from you. You should be having fun. It was foolish, I realized it soon after, but I didn't want to stop you from having a chance at happiness. I decided to stay out of your way."

"I've already called you a fool, haven't I?" I smiled at him, already forgiven him for the pain and anguish he caused me. He was altruistic to a fault.

"Yea, and so did Helen. She's continually told me I was an idiot for the last three months. Today she said it was not an option. I couldn't stay away. I wanted you to know, at least why... Even if you didn't forgive me, Ash." He frowned. "Do you?"

"Duh..." I took his face in between my hands and placed a soft kiss on his lips. "You know, I do. And if you ask me nicely, I will still be your boyfriend. Nothing would make me happier."

"Ash... Will you please come back? I don't think I've ever needed someone more than you. Loved anyone as much... Please?" He sighed.

"Yes... We can talk about this after the play when you take me to dinner. We have a lot to talk about. Now come on, the show is getting ready to start." I pulled him back around the building, holding hands with the man I loved. Finally, I felt as if everything was right in the world again.

We walked back into the theatre's lobby, and I saw Sebastian standing in the corner. He raised his eyebrow at me, curiously.

I quickly kissed Jon on the cheek as he went in to take a seat beside Helen, and I walked over to Jon.

"Happy opening night," He smirked. "I take it that was…"

"Jon. Yeah…" I said slowly, not really knowing how to tell him that this thing, as small as it was, was over between us.

"You guys got back together. That's sweet," Sebastian said, putting his arm around me. "You and me, Asher… We are better off as friends, anyway, don't you think?"

"I do… What we had was nice."

"Nice… is not what either of us wanted, though, was it?" He chuckled throatily. "Honestly… I never knew you had a daddy thing. That makes me want to ask so many questions. Next time we grab drinks, you better be ready. I'm glad you're happy, Asher."

Sebastian was still as wonderful as I had always thought him. This could have been a very awkward summer if he hadn't been. We went inside and watched our show. It was an incredible night.

9

Oliver

The first weekend of Nunsense was a smashing success, and the review in The Point Pleasant Gazette was phenomenal. Everyone celebrated all weekend long, and Sebastian was right there in the middle of it all. Helen was so proud of him. It was actually really nice to watch her during the show as she beamed at what her favorite nephew had created. Well, what we all created, I should say, even if the driving force was all him.

I really wanted to dislike him.

It would be easier if I could give him the professional cold shoulder and pretend like I had never had feelings for him.

I guess getting over your first crush was an impossibility.

The problem was since he returned… Well, feelings had too. But there was little point in any of it. He didn't feel the same way, that was obvious. I had tried to tell him, to let him know… I couldn't. I was too scared of him rejecting me again. He didn't even remember the first time, all those summers ago, when he broke my heart. I would be a fool to give him that chance again. He was here on borrowed time, and these three months were just a mirage. Soon, I would be here alone again. That was easier.

"Ollie?" Sebastian walked into my small office as I was preparing to close up for the night. "Wanna go grab a drink with me? Helen has some ladies over, and I don't really wanna go home."

"We have a busy day tomorrow with Rent coming in to start rehearsals. It's probably better if we get some sleep, don't you think, boss man?" I smirked and zipped up my backpack.

"Please, Ollie? Don't make me beg..." He leaned against my desk, and I could smell him. I had to grab the desk to stop my head from spinning. He smelled like cologne and the beach. He spent all of his time lying out there in the sand when he wasn't working. He came here pale, but he was leaving very tan. It looked too good on him. It was how I always remembered him, and that stupid tan line he always had from wearing flip-flops.

I stood up straight and took a step away. He was safer from a distance.

"One drink... Okay, probably two. I'll even buy." That stupid beautiful grin slowly spread across his face, and I knew I was sunk. I couldn't say no, even if it was in my best interest.

"You sure you wouldn't rather grab a drink with Asher?" I walked past him and left him leaning there against my desk dumbly. His mouth falling open. I turned out the light and laughed. "Fine... Come on."

"Oliver... You are my hero."

That's how we wound up at Liberties Pub. I had expected to see some of the old gang hanging out here tonight, but then I remembered they would probably all be at Rumors tonight. Crystal loved drag queens. Wherever she went, the others were sure to follow.

That meant I had Sebastian to myself tonight.

That was dangerous.

Lewis, the bartender, handed me my Cloud City Ale and gave Sebastian a dirty martini, extra dirty with three olives. He sipped it gently and grinned at Lewis.

"Perfect. Thank you." Sebastian nodded. "Oh, Oliver, what are we gonna do with you. You've been smarmy all week."

"I've been normal, all week, Slim. But you've been very busy, so maybe you didn't notice." I took a sip of my beer and didn't look at him.

"Busy, huh?" he chuckled that quick-dry hiccup of a laugh he had perfected being a city boy. It was annoying. Maybe the most annoying thing about him. No... That was his fucking smile.

"Well, we did just open a show..." I responded slowly as if he were stupid. I didn't want him to know that he and Asher... Whatever that was... bothered me. That wasn't his business. Those emotions belonged to me, and I would have to work through them myself.

"I know, I... Well, Asher and I were getting to know each other and... I guess you could say we went on a few dates... But that is over, whatever it was. We are friends, Oliver. You know, like us. He and his boyfriend got back together on opening night. It was very sweet." He took another sip of his cocktail. He held the glass balanced so perfectly between his fingers, it was kind of entrancing. I would have spilled that shit all over the bar. He was a big city gay...

"You know, I know, Slim. I saw you. I think you made sure I did." I cocked an eyebrow at him. He grinned sheepishly.

"I have no idea what you're talking about, Oliver. I think you give me more credit than I deserve," he shrugged. "You know I'm hopelessly unaware."

"You can say that again..." I mumbled. He glanced over at me and turned in his stool to stare at me.

"You have something to say?" He sat his glass gently down on the bar.

"Just calling it as I've always seen it, Slim. As much as you've changed, and you have definitely changed, you are still the same in so many ways. Just as blind now as you were then." I blurted, wishing I could pull the words back.

"And what is it I am blind about Ollie? Please, oh wise one, tell me what it is I can't see," he teased, but I knew he was curious. I wondered if he had known all these years and would that make it any better or worse. At the moment, I was choosing worse for two-hundred, Alex.

"I...uh... Well, can we start with Danny? He was already taken back then even if you did have a stupid schoolboy crush." I stated flatly.

"Not fair. Everyone had a crush on Danny..." He interjected, and I held up my finger to silence him.

"Now, it's poor sad sap, Asher. Both of them were in love with someone else, and yet you pined away... You can't see what's right in front of you." I crossed my arms and tilted my head as I stared at him.

"You are what's right in front of me, Ollie," he smirked. "I have twenty-twenty."

"You must have cataracts!" I guffawed, feeling my stomach drop. He knew... maybe. That made it worse.

He leaned back in his chair and crossed his legs. "You're sitting right there..."

Like I said, blind. He still had no clue.

It was better that way, wasn't it? The wanting of Sebastian was my own cross to bear.

"Well, you got me." I picked up my drink and took a swig. "Your dating life is none of my business, thankfully."

"Yeah… I guess it really isn't." He turned back around and nodded his head as if he had something else to say. I decided to change the subject.

"You excited to start Rent rehearsals tomorrow?" I asked, not really caring one way or the other, but this was a much safer topic.

"You know it, Ollie. It's going to be something pretty fucking fantastic for this town. I feel it in my bones." He lifted his glass and took a sip.

"Are you ninety years old? Do your bones tell the weather too?" I snorted. He gave me the side-eye.

"I will say this for you, Oliver. You keep me on my toes."

He had no idea the tap dance I was doing to stay sane around him. I was a fucking ballerina.

ACT TWO

10

Chance

I had no idea when I walked into the theatre today that I was going to be directed by a fucking Bel Ami model. His name is Sebastian… Jesus. I can hear myself moaning his name in his ear as I slam myself into him. I don't usually fuck my directors. Of course, they are typically much older or women, so this was a pleasant surprise. Score one for Point Pleasant. The rest of the cast is young and good looking too, but Sebastian is going to be mine, one way or the other.

I was excited to get cast in a professional production of Rent, even if it was in the middle of no-where, USA. It was one of those shows that got me interested in becoming an actor. I usually get cast as the romantic lead in older musicals, and this was a great opportunity to stretch myself as a performer. Roger is a hard role, vocally and emotionally, and I came ready to give it my all. I was going to be laser-focused on this show and nothing else.

Then tall and sexy, walked into the room and told us that he was the director. I almost fell out of my chair. I definitely sported a woody. I'm young and horny, sue me.

I'm also used to getting exactly what I want. And Sebastian was exactly what I wanted, at least for the run of the show. I wasn't really looking to get married or anything. Boyfriends were hard when you were a theatre gypsy.

He noticed me. It happens, and I'm used to it.

I was born genetically blessed. People have told me how beautiful I am since I can first remember. At first, it felt like a curse when I was younger, but now I know it's a badge of honor. Being gorgeous hasn't hurt me, that's' for sure. It helps me get hired for modeling and acting almost every time I go to an audition. I'm six feet, two inches, jet black, wavy hair, and the face of an angel. I also have a total gym body. I work out all the time and even have a huge Instagram following of people who want my fitness tips. That means, shirtless photos, of course. I have to give the fans what they want.

We do a sing-through of the group numbers and work out some of the more intricate harmonies. I watch the director, as he takes notes while watching us sing through the score. There's very little dialogue in the show, and I think he is impressed by how I sound. I may not be the best actor in the world, but I can sing my ass off. I keep him in the corner of my eye as we rehearse. He keeps looking over at me… He must like what he sees, and that means he has to be gay. No one who looks as hot as he does is straight. And yes, I know that's not true, but let me have my lie. It makes cruising easier if I assume my prey can be had.

We get through the first act, and the musical director, calls for a twenty-minute break. I could use it. This music is tough as shit to sing, and if we're not careful, we could damage our voices singing it. I stand and stretch my arms over my head, and I can feel my shirt slide up, exposing my tight midriff. Sebastian notices too, as does a couple of other guys in the cast.

Good... I prefer to be the alpha in the room. It makes the whole experience easier if everyone knows that I'm the person they want to be friendly with.

I walk off the stage and out into the auditorium, making sure that I make definite eye contact with the director as I walk by him. I go out into the lobby and throw open the doors as I walk into the beautiful sunny day that I'm not getting to enjoy. What I really want to do is strip naked and run into that gorgeous blue lake. It's so close, yet so far away when I am stuck inside of the theatre.

"It's gorgeous, isn't it?" A nice deep voice purrs from behind me. "You ever been to The Pleasant before?"

I don't turn around. I'm sure it's him. "Gotcha," I silently mouth, smiling at the knowledge that he is probably into me. I usually assume most gay guys are. Sue me- I'm self-assured.

"Nope. First time. I'm from Denver, so I'm used to the mountains, but that lake is pretty fucking spectacular." I say calmly as if I don't care who's speaking to me. "God, it's warm out here."

I turn towards him and slowly pull off my t-shirt, making sure I am flexed for the gods as my body reveals itself. I have done this so many times, I'm a fucking master at it. I crack my neck, nonchalantly, and throw the t-shirt across my shoulders.

"Damn... Now that is nice. I think I'm going to look forward to laying out there on that beach when rehearsals are done. You ever get out on the water, Sebastian?" He nods. "I can't believe I've never been here before. This whole town is kind of mind-altering like it's an old village unchanged by time. You from here?" I sat down on the small brick wall that kept the sand at bay from the theatre's walkways.

"No... I live in New York. I'm here as a favor to my aunt this summer. You have a really nice voice. It's a very pure sound." I watched his eyes graze across my body. It was what I was hoping would happen. I worked incredibly hard to give people something beautiful to look at. Speaking of, I had to remember that this was a great place to take some photos for my fans on the Gram.

"That's cool. I've been to the city a couple times. My best friend lives in Astoria, and I've visited her a few times. She's in Frozen, right now. I've thought about moving there, but I work all the time in Denver, and it's so much more laid back." I sighed, making sure my chest fell at the right time. "We'll see. I guess I'm just looking for a reason to finally do it. Do you think it's worth it?"

"For me, yes. It's where I belong, I guess. That's a question you have to find out for yourself. It's not an easy city to live in. It's crowded, loud, and dirty." He came over and sat down a couple feet away from me. He had really nice biceps. Not as nice as mine, but nice enough.

"Yeah... That doesn't sound so bad." I said huskily, dropping my voice to a purr. "I like it like... that." I stood up and stretched my arms above my head and moaned gently. "God, that feels good. I guess I better get back inside. I've heard the director is a real hardass."

I slowly put my shirt back on. I saw him smirk in the corner of my eye. Those lips were begging me to bite them.

"Yeah... He's a real ass," Sebastian laughed. "If you're late, he punishes you with public shame."

"Now that sounds like fun. See you inside," I flirted, and yes, I know I was coming on strong, but when you know you want something, it's good to rub your stink all over it, so everyone else knows to back the fuck off.

Sebastian knew where I stood. It wouldn't be long before he let me know he was interested. It's just the way things were. They were almost always interested.

I walked back into the theatre and could see him shaking his head through the glass wall that looked out onto the beach.

Yeah…

He knew.

11

Sebastian

Rent is a bitch of a show...

Asher has his hands full with making sure everyone is on point since the show is almost an opera in scale. Liza is only doing choreography for La Vie Boheme, and the rest is staging that falls on me. For the most part, the cast is ready for the challenge. We have some vocal powerhouses, and I am shocked that Amber is more than holding her own with these singers. Most of them are more pop singers than Broadway. Amber is a legit vocalist with a gorgeous soprano voice, but she is belting her ass off with everyone else.

Chase is by far the most talented male singer in the cast. His voice really is good enough to compete in whatever city he chooses to work in, but that attitude is something else altogether. I can feel his bright green eyes follow me as I stage the show. He is stunning, that's for sure. If I had met him in New York, I would have hooked up with him in a second.

But he comes on way too strong.

Never say never, I guess. There are worse things in the world than being flirted with by a gorgeous guy. Chase is just... well, it feels like he's *chasing* me. Everywhere I turn, he just happens to be there.

"Hey, Ollie!" I shouted across the lobby as I saw him descending the stairs to the lighting booth. "I think I need to go for a drink tonight. You game?"

I saw him pause and take a deep breath. He was going to say no.

"Come on... Do not make me beg," I pleaded, flashing him a quick grin. "Just one... I need to unwind."

"Fine. But I told Crystal I would meet her at Rumors tonight. You can tag along." He said before turning and going into the office. He hadn't even said hello today. He just came in grumpy and went up to his office. Oliver worries me, and I can't really put my finger on why.

"Rumors, huh?" Chase's voice surprises me from behind, startling me and causing goose flesh all over my body. Jesus! "I might see you there. That's what I was planning on tonight too. It could be fun..."

He brushed past me and went into the bathroom.

Well, tonight should be interesting.

I went back into the auditorium and picked up the script for the show. We were staging Maureen's performance scene, and I wanted to make this as epic as it could possibly be. I looked over my notes and waited for the break to be over. By my watch, we still had ten minutes. God, I needed a drink.

Oliver had created a great special effect with the motorcycle entering, so that was going to be fantastic. All I needed to do was...

"The show's looking great, don't you think?" Chase sat down beside me. His man spread, causing his leg to rub up against mine. That was definitely purposeful. Hot, too. Fuck… this was going to be a long couple of weeks if he kept this up.

"Yeah…" I sighed quietly. His attention was nice and flattering, it made my heart beat a little faster, as attention and flirtation always do. He made me a little confused. The right choice was to ignore it. I should ignore it, shouldn't I?

Fuck.

"Are you getting what you need out of us? I felt like that last run-through of One Song Glory was… I don't know, I felt something I hadn't felt before. Thank you. Your direction was great. It felt raw and almost painful." His voice dripped with sincerity. This was a nice look on him. "You're really great at working with actors. A lot of directors I've worked with are all about the staging and don't put enough work into the individual performances. You really make us dig deep." He leaned in a little towards me. His bare shoulder underneath his tank top rubbed against mine, just for a second. I felt it in my toes, who wouldn't. Contact, heat… attraction. Sex.

Damn.

"Thanks, Chase. I appreciate that. It's great to know I'm connecting with the actors," I said carefully, keeping it as professional as possible.

"Oh, I feel like we are seriously connecting, Sebastian," he leaned in and whispered in my air. Gooseflesh shot down my spine as his hot breath tickled my neck. God, it smelled sweet. "Don't you?"

He moved slowly away from me. "I am really interested in working with you privately. I bet you could really get a great performance out of me if you wanted to." He said so seriously, I felt as if I had already asked him. "Offers on the table, Sebastian. Hope you don't think I'm coming on too strong. I just know what I want. Do you?"

Before I could even gather my thoughts to the workplace harassment I was experiencing, he stood up and let his finger run itself across my shoulder, before he walked away and went back to the stage. I was dumbfounded and completely turned on. Chase was a walking erection, and everyone with a pulse felt it when he was in the room.

Oh, I wanted to see him writhing underneath me, or me underneath him… Probably me underneath him. But opening Pandora's Box with Chase could be as terrifying as it felt. I couldn't go there. I had other feelings running through my mind for someone else, and until I could rationalize what was happening there, Chase was a no. I assumed he didn't take no, easily. I bet he did nothing easily…

Damn.

I glanced at my watch again. I had three minutes before people expected me to have my shit together. I sat there trying to get the image of a naked Chase out of my mind.

* * *

After rehearsal, I went home and showered. Helen was holding court with a couple of her lady friends, Sandra included. Having Sandra at the theatre had been a godsend. She dealt with all the travel and housing for the actors, their per diem, and the ticket sales. How did Helen do it all when it was just her running the theatre and directing the productions? My aunt's work ethic and dedication to her theatre was inspiring. I could never accomplish it all, the way she did. She was an inspiration.

I threw on a pair of shorts and a t-shirt with a rooster

Another Opening, Another Showmance

on it from my favorite bar in the city. I walked downstairs and gave her a peck on the cheek.

"Tell Oliver I said I miss him and have fun, honey. I'm glad rehearsals are going so well. I can't wait to see Rent." She patted me n the cheek. "Go get laid. You've been too tense lately."

I pretended to be shocked, dropping my jaw open in surprise. "Aunt Helen!" I exclaimed, clutching the invisible pearls around my neck.

She cackled and smirked at me.

"I'm too tired, anyway. Besides, Oliver is so not interested in me, so I think that's off the table." I shrugged.

"Stranger things have occurred, dear. You and Oliver would be so good for each other. He would ground you, and I've always said you needed that. Of course, the man you are now is not the same little boy with his head in the clouds. I miss him." She sighed and lifted her glass of red wine into the air. "Here's to growth, which really just means getting older."

"No shit," Sandra barked. "The last time I grew as a person, I turned fifty. Worst day of my life."

"Go one and get out of here. Have fun, honey," Helen said sweetly, her eyes glowing with the love she had for me. Every day with her was absolutely wonderful. I loved sitting up with her and talking until it was later than we planned. I could get used to this.

"See you tomorrow, Sebastian. If you see Evan tonight, please tell him I want a grandbaby." She said seriously.

"I will deliver the message if I run into him. However, I think it's just Crystal and Oliver I'll be seeing tonight. I think she's trying to help get him out of that hard-crustacean shell of his," I answered snidely. It was true. Oliver was a hard nut to crack, and I had been trying. He was a gentle giant, and there were moments when I really hoped we were connecting. Then he would say something acidic or confounding, and I felt like we had taken two steps back instead of a step forward.

I hopped in Helen's car and drove to Rumors. I had met Danny and Blake here once already, so I knew where it was. I knew where everything in the Pleasant was. It wasn't hard.

I walked past the doorman, who just nodded at me and saw Oliver and Crystal over by the bar talking to the bartender. I waved as I walked up.

"Slim! Glad you could join us. Ollie here was telling me how hard you all have been working. I loved Nunsense. It was fucking hilarious. But I have listened to the Rent soundtrack my entire life. I can't wait." Crystal gushed, as she moved her bag out of the way to make room for me between her and Oliver.

I sat down and put my elbows up on the bar.

"Hey, Bruce..." Oliver called to the bartender. "He will have a dirty martini, four olives, and could you use the Grey Goose, please."

I looked over at Oliver and nudged him with my elbow. He frowned at me, but the edges f his lips told me he didn't mean it.

"You remembered. Thank you, Ollie." I said sweetly, laying it on a little thick.

"It's not hard to remember, Slim. Once I knew you liked it dirty... It was hard to forget." His laugh lit up his face. I stared at him and was once again struck by how handsome he was. It was hard to reconcile that college student with acne, to this strong and virile man. He hadn't shaven in a couple days, and I really wanted to reach up and feel it against my fingers. I also liked my fingers and was afraid Oliver might break them if I did that.

"So, Oliver was telling me that you have a shadow." Crystal's voice was heavy with off-color meaning.

"I have something… I have never been so… I mean, I think I now know how the popular girl in high school felt. He comes on very strong." I thanked the bartender as he set my glass in front of me.

"You haven't squashed his behavior yet. I think you like it," Oliver said, tightening his lips to stop himself from smiling. "I've seen him in action from the lighting booth. He zeroes in on you and can't stop himself from touching you."

"Is he hot?" Crystal said hopefully. I couldn't see what Oliver did on the other side of me, but it made Crystal laugh. "Really? That hot, huh?"

"Yeah… He's a walking and talking porn star come to life. If I had met this dude two months ago, I would have jumped in bed with him when we met." I frowned. "I was shallower then." Crystal laughed.

"What's stopping you, Slim?" Oliver said quietly. "It doesn't look to me like you dislike it. You've always had a thing for pretty boys, haven't you?"

I turned and looked at him. Damn, he could be biting when he wanted to.

"Lots of things, Ollie." I cocked my head and narrowed my eyes at him. "And I do not have a thing for pretty boys. I want someone who… you know, gets me and… Speaking of getting me, Oliver. You confuse the fuck out of me. One minute I think we are getting along so well, and the next you… Just twist the knife. Sometimes I think you really dislike me."

I wish I could take it back, but he just gets under my skin so badly it itches until I can't handle it anymore. His eyes harden.

"I could never hate you, Slim. Once again, you have

shown that you don't get it at all." He seethed at me, and it made me wilt on my stool.

Crystal whistled. "You two... It never changes... Does it?"

Before I could reply, we were interrupted by a hand on my shoulder. Oliver snorted. It was not one of the cutest things about him if I were being honest.

"Wow... Here we are. Isn't it great to let loose and be around each other besides in the theatre? A couple of the other cast members are over there in the corner, talking about their favorite Broadway divas. So far, Patti is beating Bernadette. Hi... I don't think we have officially met. I'm Chase." He offered his hand and literally put himself between Oliver and I. Crystal's eyes widened.

Oliver stared at me a moment longer and then offered his hand. "Oliver. I'm the..."

"Technical director and designer, I know." Chase's voice dropped low as if he had admiration for him.

"I'm Crystal. Who the fuck are you?" Crystal boomed loudly enough for other people to snicker in our vicinity. Fuck, I have missed her. Isn't it funny how you don't remember how much you love someone until you are with them again? Crystal was that kind of person. I wouldn't forget again. She was a fucking riot and always had been.

"Oh! Sorry," he said, throwing his arm around me and hanging off me as he sauntered over to my other side to talk to Crystal. I felt like a piece of meat. But watching Oliver's face was priceless. I couldn't tell what emotions were washing through him, but it was like watching a David Lynch film. It was riveting. "Hi. I'm Chase. I'm in Rent over at the playhouse."

"Charmed... I'm sure." Crystal held out her hand like some 1940's femme fatale. Chase took it in his hand, and to his credit, even kissed it. He was not thrown off easily, it seemed. He could roll with the punches. Crystal glanced around Chase and winked at me. "I'm a fucking lady, bitches."

"So, how do you know these two?" Chase gave her a dazzling smile.

"We all grew up together, I guess you could say. It's kind of complicated. We were summer buddies. Of course, Ollie and I went to school together, but Slim here, he was a summer delight." She cooed, knowing it was driving both Ollie and me crazy. She was egging Chase on. She couldn't help herself. "Besides, a lady, like myself, likes to surround herself with as many hot gay men as she can find. It's really all life has to offer, don't you think, Chase?"

"Oh, I agree. I've been surrounding myself with hot gay men since I hit puberty. Sebastian here is a prime specimen." He dropped his voice. "Oliver is too. But he's a little too butch for my taste. I like them refined and beautiful. Are you guys going to dance?"

"It's a school night, Chase. I think we were just about to head out for dinner, weren't we fellas?" Crystal said, overly sweet. Oliver snorted. I nodded, playing along. I had to admit, seeing Chase in public was even scarier than in the theatre. I felt like he was about to straddle me and suck my face into his.

"Well, that's no fun," Chase pouted. "I was hoping to see your moves on the dance floor."

"Another time, I guess. We have a long day tomorrow." I said seriously.

"Then I will see you in the morning. I promise I'll keep everyone in line tonight." He bent down and whispered in my ear. Kissed my cheek gently and walked away back to his castmates.

"Holy shit…" Crystal's opened her mouth, trying to find her next words. "That was…"

"Frustrating," Oliver answered, his voice tight.

"And kind of hot... Come on. Let's go have one last drink at Liberties. I want some cheese fries." She got up and waited for me to down my drink.

I could feel Chase's eyes following me out of the door.

12

Oliver

"Hey Ollie," Crystal smiled at me as I walked into Margie's. It was the end of the day, and rehearsal today was loud, and Sebastian kept stopping and yelling every ten minutes on the fucking dot. I needed something to soothe my nerves, and Crystal was just the shoulder I needed. Besides Helen, she was the only shoulder I had, and I could not talk to Helen about what I was feeling.

Hell, I wasn't sure I could even really talk to Crystal about it. She knew a lot of what I was going through back then, but she didn't know it all. No one did.

"Hey, doll. Hope you don't mind a little company for a bit. I needed to decompress after a long day, and your cinnamon bun sounded like just the thing." I plopped down on the stool and let the stress of the day slowly roll off of me.

"Slim being a pain in the ass today? Or was it that hunky actor? Jesus, he was a handful. Is he still fawning all over Slim?" She pulled a giant pastry out of the glass case and put in her toaster oven to warm it up exactly how I liked it.

"Yes. Yes. And yes, to all of the above. Can I get a coffee too, Crystal? I am going to have to go back to the theatre tonight and try to finish the damn railing before rehearsal tomorrow. Sebastian kept yelling about it all day today." I groaned. "I swear I was ready to throw a hammer at his head by the end of rehearsal. If he would have rehearsed in the damn rehearsal room today, me and my guys could have had most of everything finished. But herr director needed them to be onstage. At least, now that Nunsense is closing, we won't have to keep taking it down every night. So that will help."

"You want extra leaded, Ollie? I warn you, it will make you buzz. But I think you could use it if you have to work late tonight. Can you stay around for a bit? Dylan is supposed to drop by before he heads back to Allyria tomorrow. I miss that little shit, and I'm sure he would love to see you." She said, grinding the beans for my coffee. I loved the way he stuck her tongue in the corner of her mouth when she was concentrating. It was one of those funny little traits you find comfort in with your friends.

"Sure. It's just me over there tonight, so I am on my own time."

"So, tell me about that actor. I have never in my life seen someone be so aggressive. Poor Slim... I could tell though that he was not really into him. I think he has other things on his mind, Ollie. Does it still bother you? I think it does." She set a cup under her espresso machine and started the drip. The aroma of the beans filled the air.

I could feel my shoulders sag, and something broke within me. I could feel the words bubbling up before I could stop them. "More than you know."

"After all this time, Ollie... You still feel the same way, don't you?" She leaned across the counter and took my hand in hers, offering me comfort. She knew how broken I was after that summer. She never told me she knew why, but she made sure to include me as often as I would let her.

"I don't want to… I just… I mean, how can I ever tell him, Crystal? He doesn't even remember or even know what that summer did to me. What he did… without even… I was so broken, and I will never let myself become that person again. To feel that again, you know?" I dropped my head and stared at the counter. Her eyes were too concerned, and I couldn't take it. "How can you love someone, so much, and be afraid of loving them?"

She sighed heavily and walked back over to her machine. She started making my coffee and poured some milk into her small metal pot before steaming it.

"Ollie… You know that I know loss. Losing Wyatt almost broke me in high school and then finding out I was pregnant with his… The last piece of him on this planet was growing inside me. I gave it away because that was what was best for her… Hell, for me. But it took me years to slowly tear down the walls I built around my heart." She turned off the machine and poured the milk on top of my coffee. "Poor Larry… I wish I would have told him that I was… the mess I was, before we… you know… I was so scared of falling in love again, and having my heart destroyed all over again by someone else, that I didn't allow myself to feel the emotions that were raging inside me. I love Larry. I do. But he also knows I can never fully give myself to him. So, we have what we have. We have our ups, and we have our downs, and sometimes we just ride the calm still waters of us, together, and that is enough." She slid my coffee over to me after stirring it. "You deserve your chance at enough to, Ollie. Sebastian is not the same silly boy he was then, and neither are you. You're both grown men with baggage, sure. But you have also both grown and are stronger than you were then. You deserve to tell him your truth, and he deserves to hear it. Not that I blame him, understand. I really don't think he knew, Ollie. And the way he… Well, I think you should see where it leads if you let him in…"

I felt heavy. I knew everything she was talking about. Her boyfriend Wyatt died in a car crash, and for some reason, Crystal has always said it was her fault, even if she wasn't in the car. I wasn't with them that night in high school. I wasn't the kind of kid to go get drunk in fields back then. Sometimes I wondered what my life would have been like if I had been able to let down my guard and just allowed myself to be the awkward person I was. To Crystal and the gang's credit, they always treated me kindly. Gay people stuck together in The Pleasant.

"I don't think I can do that, Crystal. But I know…" I started, and she put her hand back on mine.

"I'm okay, Ollie. This is about you. Happiness is fleeting, my friend and we find it in the strangest places. Who would have thought Larry would make me happy? I couldn't stand him once upon a time. But life has a way of giving you exactly what you need when you need it, and maybe Slim has walked back into yours for a reason. Want something more, honey. You deserve it." She was so sincere I could feel my emotions bubbling to the surface, and before I knew it, tears were rolling down my face. I buried my face in my hands, and in a few seconds, I could feel her arms reach around me from behind, and she pulled me into her. I turned around on the stool and let the sobs come. My toes curled as my emotions lashed out of me and onto Crystal's warm shoulder. Her hand stroked my head, and I melted into her.

I don't know if it was a minute or an hour, but I eventually felt my tears dry up, and I composed myself as best I could. The walls were back, and I was safe. But I was not the same. Something she said had taken root in me. I did want something more… I just wasn't sure I could handle it if he didn't feel the same way. Why would he?

"Thanks, Crystal," I managed to say as I wiped my face with my t-shirt.

"Anytime, Ollie. You are my friend, and I will always be here for you. You can count on that, honey. I take care of my gay boys, and you all take care of me." She sat down beside me. "I'm glad you let us have this talk, Ollie, and if you ever want to talk about it more… You know I am here, okay?"

"Okay."

The door opened, and Dylan walked in flanked by his bodyguard. He smiled as we turned, but it was strained. Something was off with Dylan.

"Peyton? Can I please have a little time with my friends?" The bodyguard nodded and stood by the door at attention. It was alarming.

"Hey Dylan," I said, hoping I didn't look like I just had a cry-fest. I could feel my eyes burning, so I was sure they were red as shit.

"Oliver." He hugged me. "I'm glad I got to see you again. My parents have been keeping me busy. I wanted them to feel as if they were a part of planning this monster wedding. Jesus, I can't wait for it to be over."

He sat down in a chair in front of us.

"Still as crazy as ever, I see…" Crystal said snidely. "Really, Dylan… This does have to stop eventually, right?"

"According to Liam, the whirlwind has just begun. But hopefully, this part of it will be at an end soon. The Queen has put every resource at her fingertips on it, so with any luck, I won't have to be followed by the incredible hulk forever." He sighed, and I could see the weight on his shoulders. Worry sat there like a badge of honor.

"Dylan? What is happening? I'm sorry… Maybe you don't want to…" I began, and he held up a hand and glanced over at Crystal, who nodded.

"It's okay, Ollie… I think it will be good to confess it to someone else, but let's keep it to ourselves, okay. I don't want everyone calling worried about me all the time," he said quietly, running his hands through his strawberry blonde hair. "Danny will fly to Allyria and never leave, and that will not help the situation."

"Tell him…" Crystal egged him on.

"It all started with a letter arriving at the palace and Liam and I hearing the queen scream…"

I couldn't believe my ears. By the time he told me his tale, I was worried that this would be the last time I would ever see my friend. His life was in danger.

13

Chase

Rent finally opens in two days. We've been rehearsing non-stop, and Sebastian's been a hard taskmaster. To his credit, this show is the best thing I have ever been a part of in my life. The entire cast gets emotional during the show because Sebastian has helped every one of us dig to be the best we can possibly be.

He's fucking hot as hell, but he is also a damn good director. No wonder his New York reviews are glowing. He's the real deal, and I hope to ride him all the way to the city. Having someone like Sebastian on my side will only help my career. Of course, I am also madly attracted to him, and that is driving me crazy.

He flirts with me. He treats me nicely, and whenever I'm around, he blushes, so I know he's thinking what I'm thinking. We make sense… So why shouldn't we get naked and treat each other like we hate each other? God… He is driving me crazy. I would have thought I would have pounded him by now, but he is playing hard to get. Maybe he's just waiting for the show to open before he shows me how much he's attracted to me? I don't think I can be anymore honest in what I want with him. I've been coming on strong, and he is still keeping me at bay.

Fuck. I'm horny as hell.

Whatever... I am exhausted with rehearsals, and we finally have a day off, since we are now in technical rehearsals in the afternoon and night, so I decided to go to the beach. This is where I will be spending my days from now on out.

It's a gorgeous day, and the sun is baking the hot sand. I'm glad I wore my flip flops today. The theatre has put us up in a small row of houses that sit behind the theatre. Each small house is divided into four bedrooms with a shared kitchen and bathroom. It's a lot like dorm living. It sucks. But at least the other three guys I live with are quiet and clean. We hang out every now and then, but today I wanted to be alone.

There are a lot of people on the beach today. For two weeks, I have stared at the crowded beach and wished I had some free time in the day to join them. Today I wish it wasn't so crowded. I pull my shirt off and throw it over my shoulder. I have my towel and sunscreen in my hand, and I walk down among the many sunbathers and wind my way between them.

Damn, the water looks great. I'll have to jump in after I bake in the sun for a while. I really need a tan. I still have my winter color, and I have never been a fan of pasty white skin. I get really brown in the summer, and that's how I prefer it. Maybe I should move to LA where I can stay tan all year long?

I find a spot that's not as crowded as the rest of the beach and throw my towel down on the sand. Before I sit down on it, I notice a familiar face about twenty feet to my right.

Sebastian...

He hasn't seen me. This is going to be fun.

I pick up my towel and slowly move backward until I am behind him, and I sneak upon him. He is lying back down on his towel, flipping over to bathe his chest and face with the sun's bright rays. I think better about jumping on top of him, even if it is what I want to do badly. What would he do if I just laid down on top of him, my chest rubbing against his sweaty greased-up body?

Fuck… He is gorgeous. That body is legit in great shape. He's as much of a gym bunny as I am, it seems. His pecs and abs are cut, and the ridges of his hard muscles shadow in the sun. He is breathtaking. I've had lots of breath-taking guys in my time, but Sebastian is special. I'm drawn to him, not just for what he could do for my career, I mean, it never hurts to hitch your wagon to a rising star, but there's more than that. He calls to me… I feel this incessant need to touch him, kiss him… I want to know him in the raunchiest of ways, and then get to know what actually makes him tick. And, yes, in that order.

I decide it's best to just walk over and wait for him to feel my presence. I creep up until my feet are almost beside his head and wait. My body is casting a small shadow across his face, it shouldn't take long for him to notice.

But it does. I am standing there waiting for what felt like hours, even though it was probably two minutes, but I drank in the visual beauty of his body and face while I stood there. His, uh… very small and tight bathing suit wasn't bad to look at either. Sebastian was packing, and that was starting to make me way too horny, so I lowly cleared my throat.

He opened his eyes, and I knew the first thing he saw was my crotch bulging in my speedo right above his face. I was glad this was the suit I wore. It was like a second skin, and I knew Sebastian was getting a view of everything I had to offer. A slow smile appeared, and I winked at him.

"Enjoying the view? I was worried it might block your rays…" I teased, shaking my hips slowly, making sure he noticed the ample size of my package.

"You are too much." His laugh was like a small tinkle. Musical and vibrant with mischief. "Decided to get some sun, huh? Me too. It's hard being locked inside when this is how I have always remembered The Pleasant. I love this beach."

"You mind if I claim some sand by you?" I asked, spreading my towel right against his. If he minded the invasion of his space, he would have to tell me. I wanted to be as close as I could possibly get. When God gives you a gift, you don't ignore it, and today he blessed me.

"Sure. Why not?" he raised himself up a little on his elbows, his body tightening as he held himself up. Thank you, Jesus.

I felt a twinge in my crotch. I wanted him so fucking bad, and we hadn't had a real opportunity to just be alone together. Now was my chance.

I sat down close to him, he didn't move away. I pulled out my dark tanning sunscreen, and poured some onto my legs and massaged it in, slowly. He watched me, not saying a word. It was nice just to be near him, here in this most beautiful of places.

"Sebastian? Would you mind helping me with the rest? I don't wanna burn anywhere. That would fucking suck before opening. Made that mistake once at Colorado Shakespeare, and I winced every time I moved. You mind?" I offered him my bottle, and he nodded, slowly sitting up and turning towards me. I moved so he could get the back first. I felt the slow trickle of oil hit my skin and had to stop from moaning as his hands gently yet firmly rubbed the oil over my hard muscular back and shoulders. He worked the oil down my back, letting his fingers linger over my lower back, where my tight speedo met my skin.

Fuck if this were a nude beach, he would have to touch my bubble butt… I really wanted to feel his hands slide over my mounds, I tightened them instinctively as I thought about it, letting a small moan escape my lips.

"Feels good, huh?" he chuckled lightly. "I always liked this too."

"I'll be happy to rub some lotion wherever you want, Sebastian. I'm very good with my hands if you want a beach massage. I'm sure you're tense as fuck with the show opening. I paid my way through college, giving massages. I'm really good at working all the tension out of your body." I offered, hoping he would take me up on it. He really could use it, and I could use the chance to run my fingers over his body. It wasn't something that I was either proud of or ashamed of, but I didn't usually tell people that fact about my college life. It started out pure enough, but after a few months of doing massage, I realized I could get paid a lot more doing them nude. I found out how much more I could make if I let them touch me, lick me, and eventually suck me. I even pounded some ass for a thousand eventually, but only to a couple high-end clients that could afford that kind of service. I never saw myself as a prostitute or an escort back then, but now, I know that's exactly what I was.

Look, I was young and needed the money. I got a scholarship to the vocal department, but I still had to pay for food, lodging, and books. I did what I had to, and I have no regrets. But I don't want to ever have to do it again. When you look like me, people will pay you for almost anything. Maybe I should have just been a pool boy, but in Colorado, that's not a very good option.

"There… And maybe on the massage. My shoulders really are tight, but I want you to enjoy your day too, Chase." He said, handing me the bottle of oil before starting to lay back down.

"You mind doing my chest too, Sebastian? I always make it spotty, cause I can't see if I get it all," I laid down on my back, my hands behind my head. I saw him smirk before picking the bottle back up.

"Are you always high maintenance?" He winked at me, and my heart beat a little faster. The oil was warm from the sun as it splattered on my chest. His hands explored every ridge of my body as he worked the oil over my large pecs and rippled abs. His finger twirled in my treasure trail as he massaged the oil to the line of my speedo. I moved my hands and carefully pulled the fabric down a little, exposing the briefest glimpse of my dark pubic hair. He sighed as his fingers pushed the oil carefully onto the exposed skin. "Anywhere else?" he huffed a little.

"Yeah… Under my arms a little if you don't mind?" I put my hands back behind my head, and he slowly oiled up the underside of my biceps and armpits. The dark hair gleamed in the sun as the oil clung to it. I noticed his eyes raked themselves over my body. It glistened as the sun's rays reflected off my oiled torso.

"Okay, I think you're good." He put the cap on the bottle and threw it down to the bottom of my red towel. He lay down on his back again and picked up his sunglasses and put them over his eyes. It was bright as shit out here. I should have brought my sunglasses too.

"Thanks, Sebastian. It's been nice working with you and getting to know you. I didn't think we were ever going to get some time together, alone." I glanced over at him. His lats made me want to reach out and touch them…

"Well, here we are." He turned over on his side and

propped his head up with his elbow. It was a glorious sight. He was a vision, and I drank him in deeply. "Are you always so… I mean, you come on really strong. Are you always such an alpha male?"

I turned to face him, and we lay there in a mirror image of each other. I winked. "I'm an Aries. Aggressive is just in my nature. You don't really seem to mind, though."

He sighed gently, studying me as if he were trying to decide what he should do next. I hoped it was placing his lips against mine, but he wasn't a dominant type, that was obvious. It's how I knew he was mainly a bottom. I grinned at the thought of him underneath me.

"I… don't mind… Honestly, it's nice feeling attractive again. It's been a rough year in the love department for me. I had a break up before my last show, and it left me feeling a bit uneasy about dating. I wasn't sure if it was me or the guys I was attracted to, you know. My last boyfriend was an investment banker, and the only thing we had in common was sex. That never works out." He kept his eyes focused on mine as well as he could, but I could see them dart to my chest every now and then, even though his dark glasses hid his eyes.

"So, it was amicable, or did one of you get their heart broken?" I asked, finally getting to see a side of him that he hadn't shared with everyone. This was special, this was for me.

"I guess we are still friendly… It wasn't really dramatic or anything. We were having brunch and had nothing to say to each other. We ended it there and walked away happy, for the most part. But it did leave me wondering why I always seem to choose the wrong men." He laid his arm down and rested his head against it, staring at me. "I bet you leave a trail of broken hearts behind you. If your flirting with me is any indication."

"That's what you think, huh?" I said slowly. He wasn't wrong in some ways. "I think I go after what I want, when I want it, Sebastian. Life is too short for could have beens. You have to seize the moment. I mean, I'm young and the hottest I am probably ever going to be, so why not? At least, I am honest with the people I fuck or date... But when I find the right guy... I think I could be monogamous. It's not like I haven't ever done it, you know." I paused and thought about whether or not I wanted to share the story. "Right after college, I was hired to sing on a cruise ship, and there was this guy... He was beautiful and was the drummer for the band on the ship. Talk about a ripped fucking torso. The moment I saw him with his shirt off, I fell head over heels in love. I dated in college, but it was never really anything serious. I wasn't in the space for a relationship, you know?"

He nodded, and I licked my lips. It was hot... Fuck, I should have brought some water.

"So he pursued me, right off the bat. I knew it was because of how I looked. It's always been that way for me, so I knew it wasn't deep. But he led me to believe after many nights of wild and kinky sex that we had the opportunity to be more. At the end of the contract, and I mean, we spent every moment together on the boat, but when I was done with the job... Well, he stayed, of course. And I was devastated. I put up some walls after that, and it takes me a little while to lower them. But there has never been anyone like him since. Who knows? Maybe the next hot drummer is right in front of me? Maybe not? But I am always looking and ready to grab life by the fucking reins, Sebastian. How about you? You ready to see what the future holds?"

"I think I might be..." He said, and I leaned in and grabbed him behind the head and placed my lips against his. They were soft and luxurious, but before I could really kiss him, a voice broke our reverie.

"Sebastian!" He broke away and turned to the deep voice calling his name.

"Danny, hey," he cleared his throat and answered huskily. That's when I saw it. Danny was his drummer. Danny was fucking hotter than just about any other human being I had ever met. Those dark chocolate curls and ripped body… He made me look ugly compared to him. Shit… And he was a lifeguard… Double shit.

"Hey, I'm working today and over at the station. You want to come and sit with me for a while. It would be great to catch up one on one." The hunky lifeguard said. Even his voice gave me a hardon. Sebastian was lost to me, for now. But I had made in inroad to him. He was willing… So was I.

"Sure. Sounds great. Sorry, Chase… See you tonight, okay. Do not get sunburned." He stood up and grabbed his stuff.

"Gotcha, boss man. See you later, Sebastian, and it was nice…" I grinned.

"Yes… It was, Chase," he said before walking off.

One way or another, I was going to get him to take a chance on Chance.

God, I hate puns.

14

Sebastian

R ent has opened, and it has been a crazy couple of days.

After that few hours off, when I went to the beach, the last couple of days have been spent inside dealing with any and all technical problems the show was experiencing. Oliver was brilliant. He went through the cues with the backstage staff like a drill sergeant. Any issue came up, he was right there fixing the problem before I could even offer a suggestion. I hate to say it, but he is way too talented to be stuck here in The Pleasant. His skills deserve a chance to be seen by the larger theatre community. Watching him take charge like that… It really made me see him and the man he had become.

Oliver… I hadn't been able to get him out of my mind. He was frustrating and complicated and sexier than should be possible. The gangly kid had turned into a virile and handsome man with a body I just wanted to explore with every part of my own. Why had it taken me so long to see it?

I guess it didn't really matter. He still showed plenty of

disdain for me, so I didn't have a chance, to explore this attraction with him anyway. We fit together… We made sense. Of course, he would never see that, and I was leaving in five to six weeks, so…

What could have been will probably always be just that. A coulda, shoulda…

I let Asher's sweetness and need sweep me along for a bit, and my anger at Oliver and his contempt for what was happening with us only spurred it on. Then Chase came along, and a lot of my attention was focused on trying to avoid or figure him out. There is a lot more to him than I first thought. But I should never have let that kiss happen. As beautiful as he is, as talented as he is… He is not my match. Sure, we would have crazy hot sex, probably… But I've done that already. If I'm going to invest in someone, it has to be more than that.

I shouldn't have let him kiss me, but I just got swept up in the moment. The sun shining on his muscular body, and his opening up to me… I got lost in the moment, and if it wasn't for Danny, who knows what I may have done. I would like to think I would have regained control of my libido, but…

Chase was a work of art. Everything about his physical presence was like a sculptor brought his vision of male strength and beauty to life in marble or stone. Chase was an ideal that couldn't be lived up to by almost anyone besides Danny.

It was funny to sit in his lifeguard shack with him, our feet dangling off the tower as we stared at the calm waters, and the people enjoying them for the hour we were together. I used to be so in awe of him. I didn't know when I was younger if I was in love with him or just wanted to be him. Maybe it was a little of both. Now, we are so different, so much more mature than we were, that those thoughts and feelings are better left in the past. He is even more beautiful now. The boy has fallen away, and he is an amazing man.

Much like Ollie.

It's odd… What I felt for Danny then, I kind of feel for Ollie, now. What the fuck does that mean?

Once again, I find myself falling for the unavailable person in my near vicinity. It's maddening, and I can't wrap my head around it, but I also couldn't stop myself from watching him. WE have drinks together almost every night, but he is so distant it sometimes feels as if I'm sitting alone near a stranger instead of the man I long to reach out and touch. How can I close this distance between us? Maybe I should just come clean and tell him how I feel, but we still have weeks of working together, and I know how badly that can go.

The show went remarkably well. Every technical element went smoothly, the cast was as brilliant as they could ever be, and the band, under Asher's direction, sounded as if they had been playing together for years. Maybe they have. Helen was jubilant with her praise for the show. She teared up as she saw me and it made me misty too. Dammit, I love that woman. I wish we could be closer… Or I could have more time to visit here, more often… I could easily settle here in The pleasant and do what Blake does when he has a job. New York has lost a little of its luster for me. When I first got here, I couldn't wait to get back. Now, I am looking ta extending my trip until my agent has a real reason for me to return. I could sublet my place until then…

Helen could use the help, even though I have been way to busy to be much of assistance to her, except for the theatre. Maybe she would like me to stay too. I'm sure she would. I think I would too.

Another Opening, Another Showmance

After a round of champagne at the closing night party, I got in my car to meet the gang at Rumors. I was sure a lot of the cast would come here tonight too since it was disco night. They deserved to blow off some steam, even if they had three more shows before a well-deserved break. In a week, we would start rehearsals for Noises Off, and that was going to be a welcome break from music and dance rehearsals. I enjoyed musicals, but the non-musical theatre was what I loved. Working with Blake was sure to be fun. I really liked him, and he made Danny smile as I had never seen him smile before.

Hopefully, they would be here tonight too.

I got out of my car and walked into the crowded bar. I spotted Crystal with Sam and Hunter. I waved over at them and walked up to the bar to order a drink.

"We have to stop meeting like this," Oliver said, surprising me. I turned and grinned at him, happy to see him. His tight t-shirt hugged his body, and his biceps looked like they might rip the shirt apart. Damn, he was beautiful. A small tuft of hair showing through the v-neck, and I wanted to reach out and touch it. He was so manly, and the fact he was handy made him even more attractive. I had seen what he could do with his hands, and I was impressed.

"I think I like meeting you like this, Ollie." I chatted happily. "You changed out of your work t-shirt. I liked the button up, but I think I prefer you like this."

He stared at me, dumbfounded, and a blush crept up his cheeks.

"You have a preference, do you? That's interesting." He ran his fingers through his hair and smirked. Damn… Yeah… I definitely had a thing for him. I needed to just admit it, to myself and to him.

"Yes… I think I do, Ollie," I sighed, shaking my head,

surprised by how transparent I was being with him. "You are…" I nodded. "pretty fucking amazing, actually."

"Sorry… I don't think I heard you correctly. Can you say that again?" He raised his eyebrows in surprise.

"I said you were pretty *fucking* amazing," I repeated slowly, letting my words sit before I said anything else. He looked down at the floor for a second before making eye contact with me again.

"Thank you…" He blushed again. I could get used to that. "I think you know…"

"Boys! Get your asses over here," Crystal bellowed.

Oliver turned and waved at her before turning back to me. "Yeah…"

The bartender came over, and of course, Oliver knew him. He ordered both of our drinks, and I smiled when he remembered the four olives. He really did pay attention, but is that because of him having a good memory or because he made a mental note of what I liked. Fuck… I hated having questions about him.

"Here you go, princess," he teased. "You ready to wade into the deep end with Crystal and the gang?"

"I suppose we should… But I was kind of enjoying being here with you," I stated seriously.

"Okay, Sebastian… You're too nice. What's happening here?" Oliver sat his drink down on the bar and stared at me.

"I…" and before I could say a thing. A hand smacked my ass.

I turned around to find Chase a few inches from my face. "Can I please have my kiss now, Mister Director? I don't think we will get interrupted now. You don't mind, do you?" he tossed over at Oliver.

I glanced at Oliver, trying to say HELP ME, but all I saw was his crestfallen face. That could only mean one thing, couldn't it. He felt the same way for me as I felt for him. I looked between him and Chase for a second before pulling Oliver into me and kissing him passionately on the mouth before I could even think about what I was doing.

His mouth hungrily kissed me back, and I leaned into him, completely forgetting where we were or who was around. I felt Chase disappear, and I felt bad about what I had done, but I couldn't stop it. This was what I needed, and here I was playing tonsil hockey with the man I couldn't stop thinking about, a man I would have never thought I would fall for. Here we were.

A pair of hands pushed me backward, and I almost stumbled. It was Oliver, and the look on his face froze me in place.

"Do you have any idea how cruel that was?" He spat before he walked through the small crowd and out of the bar, leaving me standing their alone, trying to make sense of what just happened.

I was stuck in place as he made his exit, my mind trying to cope with the rejection… with the kiss… his passion pouring into me… then his absence and…

What the fuck did I just do?

I walked quickly through the bar and saw him pulling away in his truck. My future felt dim.

ACT THREE

15

Oliver

We were young... I shouldn't have reacted the way I did, I know. Especially since I have wanted him to want to kiss me from the moment I met him. What do I do? I freak out, shove him backward, and ran away like a twink who just discovered Lady Gaga has a new album.

Pathetic.

I can't take it back, and I don't think I can explain it, either. I don't think I could stand the way he might look at me after.

Fuck...

It was so long ago, wasn't it?

No.

It wasn't really that long ago.

My scars hadn't fully healed. They were still raw from the sting of his rejection, the words slung in jest that he didn't think I heard. The betrayal I felt from the only one I had ever cared about.

How do you recover when your world crashed down around you at a time you were innocent and vulnerable and naïve?

Another Opening, Another Showmance

It wasn't that long ago.
It was a lifetime ago.

Seven Years Ago- The Past

"Hey Ollie, come and play with us. Why are you sitting back there all by yourself? Come on and play. Trust me, it will be more fun for you than it will be for me. Kissing gay boys isn't really going to do it for me," Crystal laughed as she stood up and pulled me down on the sand to sit in a circle with them.

Sebastian sat across from me on the other side of the circle. Danny, Hunter, Dylan, Sam, and Evan rounded out the usual suspects that sat crisscrossed, waiting for Crystal to start the game. Sam looked like he was about to lose his nerve at any moment and dash away from the group. Crystal had admitted the game could get pretty hot.

"Okay, so this is a mix of spin the bottle and truth or dare. First, the person who spins has to kiss whoever it lands on, and we are not talking about a peck on the lips. This is full-on mouth to mouth action, or it's not really fun. Then the person to the right, who will spin next, has to give a truth or dare to the couple who kissed." Everyone stared at her, wondering if she were just making these rules up for fun. Knowing Crystal, it was a possibility. But she was in charge, as she always was.

"This game sounds like a sadist made it up. It's not one; it's two games you hate to play with sex-crazed teenagers." Evan laughed, making fun of it.

"We don't have to play, Evan. Do you want to do something else?" Crystal said pointedly. Evan looked over at Danny, who nodded, and then he turned back to Crystal.

"No, it's cool. It just sounds fucked up…" He whined. "Kissing your friends is a sure-fire way to stop being friends." He laughed quietly, which made my stomach flip. If Evan was nervous, then I was fucking terrified.

"Why don't you go first, Evan? Spin the bottle, bitch." She pointed at him, asserting her control as she usually did. I adored her, but I was also scared of her. She could be a total bulldozer when she wanted. I've seen her make Hunter cry.

Evan reached out and took the bottle in his hands. He tried to hide them from shaking, and everyone pretended not to notice. Evan and I were the closest in the way we were. Fear was a dominant trait in our everyday existence. But he had Danny and had for a while. I looked over at Sebastian, and he caught my eye and gave me the thumbs up. He knew I was nervous. I wish I could have been more like he and Danny, Hunter even would have been great. They were strong and were jumped headfirst into the lake. Evan and I tip-toed in afraid of rocks.

He spun, and it twirled quickly around on the board before slowing down and landing on Hunter. Evan's eyes got big. Hunter wasn't quite as gorgeous as Danny, no one in the world seemed to be. It was like he was written by a Harlequin romance writer. But Hunter was close. He was a walking muscle, and he made your eyes fog up. That's how hot he was. I used to have a crush on him back in high school, but I knew it would always be just that. He had Kris. Had- being the operative word. He still hadn't recovered from losing him, even though he put up a good game face around everyone. But we knew.

"Come here, you sexy little twink." He wagged his eyebrows lasciviously. I didn't know eyebrows could be so dirty. We all laughed as they met over the bottle. Evan glanced at Danny, who smiled at him before he and Hunter kissed. It was a long and wet kiss that made me incredibly uncomfortable because soon that bottle would land on me, or it would be my turn to spin. I saw tongue and even heard Evan moan a little. I glanced down, and he was starting to sport a little wood in his shorts.

This game was evil.

They broke apart, and everyone giggled. "How was watching your boyfriend make out with a real man, Danny?" Hunter asked, slapping Danny hard on the shoulder.

"Hot?" he said slowly, and I knew he meant it. I looked around, and everyone's face was flushed with the rush of excitement. Mine was flushed with embarrassment. I had never kissed a boy before. Well, not even a girl really, unless you count, Katherine Ashford in second grade. I didn't.

"Danny give them the truth or dare, since you spin next," Crystal ordered.

Danny looked over at Hunter. "Truth or Dare?"

"No! You decide truth or dare for them. Just give them whatever it is." Crystal moaned. "Didn't I say that? Jesus, you queens, cannot follow the rules."

"Truth, then. Hunter and Evan, who is it you wished you had kissed," Danny said snidely, staring at the person he had always considered a brother. Things between them had been tense all summer.

"Kris… You know that, asshole." Hunter seethed.

Seven Years Ago- The Past

"You know it's you, baby," Evan reached over and kissed him gently.

"Okay... that was not very exciting, and we promised we were gonna leave Hunter alone about all of that." Crystal warned, asserting her dominance over everyone again. "Spin, bitch."

Danny held up the bottle and set it down, giving it a quick flick, and it spun harder and faster than Evan's. It slowed down and landed right between Sebastian and Sam. I saw Sebastian's eyes light up, but Sam was quicker. He chose himself as the winner and sat forward, meeting Danny in the middle.

"Close your eyes, Evan," Danny teased, grabbing Sam in an embrace, his hands plastered firmly on his ass, as he gave him a slow and deep kiss. Sam's hands reached up and twirled in Danny's hair as Danny bent Sam backward, his tongue licking along his lips before plunging in again. Okay... It was fucking hot. Sebastian was white as stone, as he sat there, looking away from the action.

Danny pulled away from Sam, who sat there on his knees for a second, before opening his eyes again. "You okay there, Sam?" Hunter laughed.

"And that my friend," Danny said to Hunter, "is how you give a man a kiss."

"Alright, stud muffin. Let's see... I think I will go truth too. Danny looked over at Hunter, and there was something in his eyes that looked like a warning. Hunter grinned and held up his hands as if to say, what? Danny did not look relaxed. "Danny and Sam. Have you two ever kissed another person when you were dating someone? Besides this game, of course."

"Yes." Sam blurted. "I kissed Dylan behind the school when I was dating Mark Richards. Dylan and I laughed

Seven Years Ago - The Past

about it afterward, but I did have a boyfriend. We were just curious. No big deal."

"I was single," Dylan said quickly.

"Danny?" Hunter grinned wickedly.

"I... uh..." Danny stammered.

"Oh, for God's sake. Yes, he has. I know, and it happened, and we have moved past it. Really Hunter... Are you trying to get back at him now." Evan said quietly.

"You knew?" Danny asked, his eyes misting a little. "Why did you never say something about it?"

"We were all drunk, and it was a gorgeous night. A little bird saw you and told me, and no, it was no one sitting here, so stop caring. We're young. Drunken kisses... are no... We are still here, right?" Evan looked around at everyone, but I notice his eyes land on Sebastian for a second longer than anyone else. "Shit happens, and you decide if it's going to define you or not. I chose to chalk it up to a mistake. Moving on now, please." Evan picked up the bottle and handed it to Hunter.

"Damn, Crystal... This game is like wicked harsh," Dylan said quietly. He was always the quiet one of the group. He thought about everything before he did it. In some ways, he was my favorite of all of them. Well, besides Sebastian. But he wasn't really a part of the group. He was a summer addition. He didn't have to live with the crew for the rest of the year.

"I don't make up the rules, gayby. It's just the way they are you all play the game how you play it. I've barely said a word," Crystal laughed. "That shit is all them. Your turn, Hunter."

Hunter looked over at Dylan. "Get ready to pucker up buttercup, cause the big man's coming your way."

"Gotta land on me first, meathead." Dylan laughed, but there was a sparkle in his eyes. Was something

Seven Years Ago- The Past

happening secretly between them? I think so, and no one in the group seemed to know. That's' what happens when you hang back on the outskirts, you see the things that they don't want you to. I was that person.

He spun the bottle, and it whirled around even faster than Danny's spin. Funnily enough, it landed on Danny.

"Oh god," Danny laughed. "Well, come on, stud. Make my toes curl."

Hunter crawled up on the person who had been his best friend for most of his life, before Kris. He and Danny had played football and soccer together forever. They were about as tight as two friends could be until Hunter and Kris broke up. Danny took that hard and still blamed Hunter for letting him go. It was all very telenovela.

He slowly lowered his head and nipped at Danny's bottom lip, taking it between his teeth and gently biting. Danny moaned a little, and then their mouths opened and their tongues intertwined. Their kiss lasted for about a minute, and Hunter was grinding himself into Danny's crotch. Danny didn't seem to mind. He was writhing underneath the larger man's hands as they found their way under Danny's shirt and explored his chest, tweaking his nipples as their kiss deepened even further.

Eventually, they broke apart. Hunter sat on top of Danny for a second before crawling off him and sitting back beside him. Danny threw his arm around Hunter's shoulders and pulled him into a hug.

"Love you, bro. Sorry I've been a fucking dick." Danny kissed the top of his head and pushed him back.

"Me too, man. Truce?" Hunter said, hopefully.

"Bros for life, bro," Danny laughed.

"Well, that was very Afterschool Special. I didn't know this game could save lives and bring people back together," Crystal moaned. However, she was happy the rift was

Seven Years Ago- The Past

finally mended. All it took was for them to make out? My friends were weird.

"Sam? What say you. Truth or dare?" Crystal said, getting the game to move onward again.

"Oh, fuck, dare. Play the rest of the game without your shirts on. I need something pretty to look at," Sam high-fived Sebastian, who glanced over at Danny to see if he was going to. Of course, he was going to. He and Hunter rarely had a shirt on in the summer anyway. They were lifeguards for fuck's sake.

Sam picked up the bottle as the boys stripped their shirt off. Hunter was more muscular than Danny but not by a lot. He was just bigger all over.

"You should have asked if they got aroused when they were making out? It was almost incest. But I bet they were both hard as a rock." Dylan giggled, and Sam applauded his wit happily.

"Oh, I'm still a little hard," Hunter grinned. "Dare me to show you, and I will."

Dylan blushed. He would like to see it, I think.

Sam spun the bottle gingerly, and it landed over on Dylan. "Pucker up bitch?" he said it so stupidly I wasn't sure they were going to kiss. It was much tamer and more chaste than the others. But that made sense. So were they.

"Dare boys," Sebastian said wickedly. He was the most like Crystal, but on him, I found it endearing. I couldn't help it, I was madly in love with him and could never tell him. Someone like him would never be with someone like me. It's not how gay hierarchy worked.

Dylan shot Sebastian a cold look, warning him that it better not be too bad.

"I dare you to take off your pants and make your butts have a conversation."

"You are an asshole," Dylan said quickly as he slapped

Seven Years Ago- The Past

Sebastian on the back of the head. He stood up. "Come on, Sam… It's not like we haven't been skinny dipping before. Show us that lilly-white redhead ass." He dropped his pants and spun around, showing us all his ass. He reached around and grabbed his cheeks and started moving them around. "Hmmm… Is Sebastian a big ass?"

Sam slowly stood up, and I could see his red pubes before he turned around and mimed with his butt cheeks. "He sure is, Dylan's butthole."

Dylan moved his ass over until it was on top of Sebastian's head. "He tastes like ass too… Mmmm… He moisturized today."

"Hey, Dylan's butthole. What do you get when you put a Sebastian in a blender?" Sam giggled.

"I don't know Sam's butthole. What do you get when you put Sebastian in a blender?" Dylan answered. He had a very pink hole, and he was spreading his cheeks so wide it was winking at us.

"Twink soup!" Sam laughed as he pulled his pants up and turned back around. Dylan did too.

"From one twink to another, buttmunch," Sebastian laughed. "I can't believe you put your ass on my head…"

"Serves you right. I barely have an ass at all, but to make an ass of you, sir," Dylan slapped Sebastian again lightly on the head.

They were pretty tight, most of the time. Tonight though, there was something else going on, and I had no clue what it was. That was rare. I knew almost everything. I knew that it was Sebastian that Danny kissed last summer. He was torn up about it and confided in Hunter. This game was fucking ruthless. Three more spins before it was my turn. Maybe they would get bored before I had to do it.

"My turn. I haven't kissed anyone all summer, so someone better get ready to pucker up." Sebastian spun

Seven Years Ago- The Past

the bottle lightly. I knew he was trying to get it to land near Danny or Hunter, cause he still carried a torch for them. Danny especially. It had always been Danny.

To my surprise, it landed smack dab on me.

Everyone ooohed. Here it was my first kiss in front of everyone. But it was with him…

My stomach dropped. The room spun, and I hadn't even moved. My ass was glued in place, and I couldn't even think of getting up to meet Sebastian halfway. He grinned and crawled over to me, knocking the bottle out of his way.

He sat on his knees and took my face gently in his hands, and then smashed himself into me. It wasn't a kiss, it was an assault of his mouth and tongue. O tried to kiss him back, but he held me in place and used me. It wasn't gentle. It didn't feel kind. It felt like he was mocking me, taking away the one moment I could never get back. He pulled away and ruffled my messy hair.

"I hope that was as good for you as it was for me, Ollie," he said as if he couldn't really care. He scooted back to his place, and I sat there, forcing myself to stay composed. All I wanted to do was cry, but I could bot do that here. I balled my fists up and felt my fingernails bite into my skin, giving me something else to feel, anything else but the betrayal I felt.

It was him. My first kiss… Was it just a joke? Was I a joke?

"I think I dare you two to go in the cave and make out for five minutes. I need a break." Dylan said offhandedly. Sebastian shot him a death stare. "Five minutes? Jesus?"

"Hey Crystal, what happens when they don't do the dare?" Dylan said sweetly.

"I think they get spanked… Hard," she whistled. "But that's a little harsh, Dylan. I know you and Sebastian are

Seven Years Ago- The Past

going through a little fit right now, and that's all fine and dandy, but Ollie here isn't a part of it."

"It's fine," I said, wanting to belong. I already felt like shit, and now I was starting to feel like a charity case. Maybe Sebastian would be nicer in the cave?

He stood up and reached out his hand to me and helped me to my feet. I felt numb as he led me into the cave. It was dark, and it took a few seconds for my eyes to adjust.

"Are you coming over here?" Sebastian asked harshly.

"Yeah…"

"We can just say we did it." Sebastian shrugged. "They don't have to know, but we should at least kiss a little, so we're not outright lying. Dylan is a fucking truth detector, trust me." He snorted.

"That was my first kiss," I said, trying to act like it didn't matter.

"Yeah?" Sebastian sounded bored. "I didn't know that. Sorry, it was so… Sorry."

"It's okay…"

"No… Come here."

I did. I walked slowly up to him, and he took me gently in his arms, bending his beautiful face down to mine and kissing me gently. His lips opening slowly as he gave me my first real kiss. His tongue slid gently between my lips, and I opened them and let him inside. I kissed him back, slowly and tentatively, but lovingly. I put my hands around his neck and gave myself over to him. My head spun with how wonderful he tasted. My mind sang with the joy I was feeling.

He slowed the kiss down and gently broke away from me, holding me and letting my head rest against his shoulder as he hugged me.

"That was your first kiss. Remember that one." His

breath was intoxicating as it blew across my face. "You're a good kid, Ollie."

"Kid? I'm the same age as you," I said as snarkily as I could.

"I'm just more mature than you. You're going to be a late bloomer, my friend. Okay, I think that is long enough, don't you?" He grabbed my hand and pulled me out back onto the beach. He bowed as we made an appearance, and we went and set back down.

The rest of the game is a haze. I don't remember who I kissed next. But everyone gave me easy truths after that. They knew.

At the end of the game, as we were getting ready to go home, I heard Sebastian whisper to Dylan. "God, I wish that had been Danny instead of fucking Oliver. I should really be mad at you right now. He's gonna follow me around forever now after I gave him his first kiss. Did you know that? Figures."

To Dylan's credit, he said nothing. Only shooting Sebastian a cold look. He never knew I heard that.

The Present Day

I never spoke to him again, even at the theatre for the rest of the summer, until he walked back into my life.

It was so long ago, but not that far away.

The scars of that night are still raw.

The kiss is still on my lips.

I am still that scared and shy, pimply-faced virgin who had never been kissed whenever I was around him.

16

Sebastian

Today has been a really shitty day, and it's only eight in the morning. I barely slept all night. I lay in bed and thought about every interaction I had ever had with Oliver in our history together, and for the life of me, I couldn't understand what his problem with me was.

I had been pushy with him since I got here. That was my job, but that wasn't it. I mean, could it be Asher? What the actual fuck...

I knew what I had to do. I needed to talk to the one person who knew everything about her gaggle of gays. I went to see Crystal. Thankfully she was alone at Margie's this morning.

"Crystal?" I said as I opened the door and saw her resting her eyes behind the counter.

"Hey, Slim... I wondered when I would see you this morning. Momma's still a little hungover." She poured two cups of coffee and walked around the counter with the steaming mugs balanced in her hands.

I took one and sat down at a table. She joined me.

"That was a surprising scene last night. You and Ollie getting into a fight… Next thing you know, cats and dogs will start getting married," she said gently, trying to let me know that it was okay. "Spill, honey."

"It wasn't really a fight… Did you see what happened? Did you talk to Ollie?" I asked, hoping she could give me some guidance. I couldn't bear the thought of seeing him tonight if we weren't okay. The fucker had worked his way into my heart, and I needed us to at least be friends, even though I think I wanted more.

"No and no… But I heard about it from a vicious little otter that used to be a twink. He has all the good gossip. So what happened? Spill all the tea for mommy, you know she needs to know so I can put you all back together again." She stared at me without judgment, easing me into telling her my sorry tale of Sebastian and the contrary knight.

"I kissed Oliver. Well, first Chase showed up and asked me to kiss him, but I didn't want to kiss him, I wanted to kiss Oliver. So, I grabbed him, and I did. I mean, I really laid one on him. My fucking toes curled, and my knee popped when he started kissing me back. He can really kiss, and he pulled me into him and then… he shoved me back and said I was cruel and ran away." I put my forehead on the table. "The problem is Crystal… I think I am actually in love with him. Like seriously… Love. I had no clue as to why I was so frustrated with him all the time, and then it hit me. I love him. I can't think straight when I'm with him. Fucking little Ollie… Well, not so little anymore… Fucking manly, Ollie and I have no idea what to do, Crystal…" I blurted all of this out in one breath.

She stared at me like I had three heads and then grinned widely. "I fucking knew it. That's why he's been so grumpy. Trust me, he feels the same way, but it's complicated, Sebastian." She sighed heavily as she weighed what to say next. "Okay... So I know."

"Please tell me, Crys," I begged. I needed to know even if it hurt me. Even if I found out he hated me. I had to know.

"Do you remember that summer after Kris and Hunter broke up? The last summer you were here, I think, and I made you all play that spin the bottle game?" she asked, looking ashamed as if she were the cause.

"Oh yeah!" I exclaimed. I had completely forgotten about that. "Dylan talked out of his asshole. I remember it a little. Why?"

"You kissed Oliver, Slim. Do you remember that?" she asked tentatively.

"Yes... Holy shit... It was his first kiss, and I made a mockery of it in front of everyone. But I didn't know. He told me about it in the cave, and I made up for it. I felt like shit about it." I said, slowly letting the memory return if even hazily. "But that's all that happened between us that night, I think... right?"

"Well... yes and no." She covered her face with her hands. "Shit, Slim... You two should really talk. Neither one of you is the same person you were then. I mean, come on... You know I loved you. We all did, but you could be a real little shit sometimes, you know. Oliver thought you hung the sun and the moon, and you always tried to get us to ditch him. He hung around because he was in love with you. Well, he was crushing on you... And I think he still is. I don't think he ever stopped, really. You could be kind of cruel to him."

I felt like the biggest piece of shit in the world. She was right. I used to make snide comments about Ollie to Crystal and Dylan all the time. To their credit, they never ditched him, even if he could be a downer every now and then. I was tired of him following me around all the time. Wherever I went, whatever I did, Oliver was always there, lurking a few steps behind me.

I mean…

Shit.

He had been around for the other summers too, but it wasn't until that last summer that he drove me crazy. We were working together and hanging out all the time, and we had nothing in common except for the fact we were both gay and into the theatre.

I also only had eyes for Danny and Hunter, and they were never really into me. They each had their own special someone. Even when Danny and I did kiss… It meant nothing to him, and he made me swear to never tell anyone. Oliver had been in my way and under my feet.

I treated him like shit that summer, except for that moment in the cave.

"Yeah… I haven't thought about that time in forever, Crystal. But you are right. I remember…"

"Apparently, Oliver heard you say something to Dylan that night when we were done being debaucherous. I don't know what it was, but it hurt him deeply. Did you even notice he never talked to you again after that night, Slim? He just stopped coming around. Dylan had to pull him back in again after you left. He was hurt, and I have felt like shit about it ever since. I should have said something to you, but I didn't. You were cool, and we were evil little bitches together. I remember some of the other things we did and turn cold when I think about them." Her honesty was like a slap in the face. I deserved it, and I knew she didn't mean it to be mean, but it hurt. I was a cruel and vicious kid. I always had been. It wasn't until that next year in college when I got my own heart broke into pieces that I started to change. I dropped the catty friends I had surrounded myself with and threw myself into classes and theatre unlike I ever had before. Art was my way of making up for the pain I had caused.

"I texted Oliver when you got here, behind the counter. He's about to walk in the door. You two need to talk." She stood up and met Oliver at the door and gave him a hug as she whispered something in his ear. She then put the closed sign on the door and walked outside.

"Slim..." Oliver said sadly. He looked like he hadn't slept much either.

"I'm sorry..." We both said at the same time.

"You have nothing to be sorry for, Oliver... You never have had anything to be sorry for. At least not with me." I hung my head. "But I do, and I didn't even realize it. It was so long ago... Well, not that long ago, I guess."

"It's felt like yesterday ever since you walked through that door. I almost quit when Helen said you were coming back to direct. But I love my job, so I didn't." He walked over and sat down on a stool by the counter. I noticed it was a safe distance from me. My heart sank.

"I'm sorry. But I am not that same asshole I was, Oliver." I placed my hands flat upon the table. The cold surface gave me some comfort. "You are also not that awkward and scared boy you once were. So what do we do? I can't help that I have feelings... Oliver, I..."

"Stop, Slim."

"Oliver... I wish you would say my name, instead of that nickname. I love it when you say it... It makes my heart leap, I swear, Ollie. I didn't kiss you last night because of... I wanted to kiss you, I have been wanting to kiss you, but I wasn't sure. I was at that moment, though, and I had the courage to do it, finally. I didn't think about it… before. I'm sorry."

"Sebastian… Stop apologizing. You did… Once was enough. I… I have held onto that memory for so long… Last night, that kiss, it unlocked it again, and I was just that scared little kid in the cave all over again." He stared at me and wring his hands. He was as nervous as I was.

I stood up and slowly approached him.

"What was it, Oliver? Tell me… I know it wasn't the cave. What was it that made you stop talking to me that summer?" I asked, knowing I needed to know it, but scared of what it would do to me. What it might do to us if there was still a chance. I knew at this moment how much I loved him, or I wouldn't be here, right now, asking this. I would have walked away and pretended like everything was okay and did the work of the theatre and left the rest alone. I needed to know what I did so I could make us whole.

"You don't want to know, Oliver. It was years ago, and I need to let the words of a little twerp go and deal with the man standing in front of me." He stared at me and stood up and took a small step towards me.

"Tell me…"

"Are you sure, Oliver?" He looked at me sadly.

"Yes…"

"You mocked me to Dylan for never having been kissed before, and you said I would never stop following you around now. You also said you wished it were Danny, but everyone knew that."

"I'm sorry… I… I wish I could take them back." I walked closer to him and held out my hand.

"Are you gonna shut up and kiss me again, or are we gonna talk ourselves to death?" Oliver spat quickly, and I flew to his arms.

I could never take back what I said, but I could make up for it now. I could let him know how special he is and how much I want to be with him.

This kiss rocked my world. Crystal kept the closed sign up until we left twenty minutes later.

That is a great friend.

17

Oliver

"So you that was a shit show if ever I saw one," I sidle up to Sebastian as he sits in the back of the theatre with his head in his hands.

"What happened? How did that happen tonight?" he moans. "That was one of the worst things I have ever seen."

"Well, when an actor falls off the stage and breaks a leg… Literally, mind you… The show can barely go on well. I thought Asher did a good job covering Mark's part, though. At least it was at the end of the act." I offer. It really was bad, though, but I'm trying to make him feel better. I know it's not working.

"At least it happened tonight. The stage manager can work Asher into the show for next weekend, over the next couple of days, while we are working on Noises Off. If this would have been yesterday…"

"The show would have gone on with Asher, just as it did tonight for the second act." I sit on the back of the seat in front of him, offering him my hand. "That poor woman, though." I snort, and Sebastian looks up at me and cackles. He laughs so hard he has to hold onto his sides.

"Her face and that scream as he landed in front of her. I thought we were going to have to call two ambulances. Oh my god… We should see if she wants to come back as our guest." Sebastian says seriously, thinking about Helen's business here in The Pleasant.

"Already done, boss man. Our house manager comped her family back for Noises Off. She's a summer staple, owns a house on the other side of the lake. I think she'll have a heart attack when Blake falls down the steps, though. We may have given her PTSD." I snort again, and he falls into another fit of giggles.

"I do want to look at that microphone stand again if you don't mind. It's still not levitating correct when Maureen moos." He stands up and leans in and gives me a kiss gently on the lips. He lingers there, his breath making me melt. He had a whiskey. It makes me want to kiss him again. So I do.

"Alright… If we keep this up, things are gonna get…"

"Hot?" I interrupted him, kissing him again, pulling him into me.

"I was gonna say messy… This being around each other and making out in every corner for the last couple of days has been driving me mad." Sebastian breathes heavily.

"My balls are sore," I admit, winking at him. "If you want… You can come and stay at my house today. I am an adult and don't live with my aunt."

"Smartass…"

"You really want to see the microphone right now…or would you rather see my microphone stand?" I growl at him as I pull him into me again. He is rock hard. So am I. "I think our decision is made."

"I can't believe we waited this long…"

"I made you wait on purpose, Slim. A boy like me won't jump into bed with just anyone." I laughed.

"Oliver… Shut up and take me home."

We hurried out the door so fast, I'm not sure we even turned the lights off.

18

Sebastian

Oliver's strong hands held me against him as he shut the door behind us. Our lips found each other's, and his tongue pushed itself needfully into mine, twisting and turning as we fought for dominance. I was sure he was going to win.

He slowly slid his hands up my shirt as he tugged it forcibly over my head, throwing it onto his hallway floor. He kicked his shoes off, and I followed suit, our mouths never breaking contact. His tongue hot and wet explored my mouth as it had often done in the last few days, but it was hotter and wetter than ever before.

His hands found the button to my jeans, and he popped it and quickly unzipped my zipper. His hand moved to cup my swollen cock in his hand as he slowly caressed and stroked it through the thin cotton that separated his hand from the heat I offered.

I fumbled with his damn belt, as I undid it and popped his button on the khakis he was wearing tonight. I started to unzip them and discovered he was not wearing underwear. I carefully finished unzipping them, and he used his legs as I used mine to get rid of the fabric separating us.

His large cock jutted out from his hard groin. The dark hair just a shadow in the dim light. I took it in my hand and was surprised by the girth of him. Damn... he was gonna put me through my paces tonight. He was a big boy... Who knew Oliver was packing this?

I pulled at his shirt, and he pulled back and took it off quickly, letting it fall into the pile of clothes at our feet.

"Upstairs, now..." He ordered, and I ran up the stairs, him close behind, his hand never leaving my ass.

When we got to the top of the stairs, I didn't know where to go, and he jerked me backward by my arm and pulled me into his room. He pushed me back onto his bed and fell on top of me. His hard cock rubbing itself against mine as he ground himself into me. His hands moved over my body, and he stuck his finger inside my mouth as he bit at my nipple.

I wanted him now. He may be all manly and aggressive, but I was still a bossy bottom, and I wrestled him until I was on top. My fingers swirling his beautiful chest hair that decorated his muscular torso.

I stood up and took off my underwear, freeing my cock from its confinement. Oliver licked his lips as he saw it. It wasn't as big as his, but it was pretty and curved a little to the left, like my brain and political leanings.

"Come here," he demanded, and I held up a finger.

"Tonight, you are mine to do with as I will, Oliver. Tonight is all about you..." I grinned at him as I crawled up and laid down on top of him, kissing him forcibly. I bit his lips, his jaw, the stubble rubbing against my face and making me burn in all the right ways.

I licked his neck, nibbled his shoulder, and made his

underarms wet with my saliva as I worshipped every inch of this man's gorgeous body.

I slowly let my tongue slide down his torso, taking my time with his small brown nipples and hard pecs. I traced every muscle with my tongue until I got to the one I really wanted. I grasped it at the base and slowly slid my tongue over its length. I swirled it around his large head before enveloping it inside my mouth.

"Seb... Fuck..." He groaned as he thrust his hips into the air, impaling me on his girth.

I let it slowly slide further inside my mouth and took as much as I could inside before he slid down my throat. I bobbed up and down on his large cock- licking, sucking, and deep throating every inch of him until he was bucking his hips wildly into me. His groans and moans music to my ears as he whispered my name.

He grabbed me by my head and started thrusting slowly into my mouth, using me for his pleasure as I became a receptacle for his love. I tasted his pre-cum as it coated my mouth, his taste both sweet and salty, and I lapped at it, savoring it as he pleasured himself, forcing my head with his hands to take every inch of him.

I couldn't take it anymore. I needed him now.

"Lube?" I asked quickly. I was on prep, so if he didn't have condoms, I wouldn't complain.

He rolled over and opened a drawer by the bed. He pulled out lube and a condom from it.

"My turn, then," he said, taking me in his arms and flipping me over until my ass was up in the air.

He spread my ass apart, and I felt his tongue dart around my hole before slowly sliding inside. He ate my ass like an all you can eat buffet in the South. It was gluttonous, and soon I was writhing in pleasure beneath him. His stubble reddening and burning my ass as he had his way with me. A finger slowly found its way inside as his tongue kept my ass wet.

I felt the trickle of the lube slide down my crack, and chills shot up my spine. It was cold, but before I could even shiver, his large finger slid all the way in as he opened me up, getting me ready for the large girth of his cock.

"Ollie, if you don't fuck me right now, I'm gonna scream. Please… Ollie…" I needed him badly. This was more than I had dreamed of. We fit together so perfectly that I couldn't imagine another man ever filling the void Ollie was sure to leave when I finally went back to the city. How could I ever…

"Aaahhh shit…" I groaned.

I felt his large helmet push itself against my tight hole as he forced himself slowly inside. Inch by inch, he filled me until I felt as if I might burst from the pressure. I would breathe, thinking he was all the way in, and there would always be another inch…

"Fuck… Seb… You are so tight, baby… So fucking tight… You feel so good, baby. So fucking hot…" He growled. I felt his pubes finally tickle my ass, and I pushed my ass back and rocked myself back and forth on his cock.

"You are a bossy little bottom, huh?" he said as he put his hand on my neck and forced my head back into the bed. Fuck I almost came right then. His asserting of his dominance over me was a fucking turn on. Most men just let me be in charge, but not Oliver. He was making me his-body, mind, and soul.

"Hold on, baby," he said as he fucking assaulted my ass. My fingers dug into his sheets, and I writhed beneath him, mewling his name over and over as he slammed into me over and over. Fast and slow, he ground his cock into my ass until I couldn't move, all I could do was whimper as he took me.

"Who the fuck... are you?" I said breathlessly as he flipped me over and threw my legs over his shoulders.

He laughed as he bent down and kissed me as his hips slammed into me over and over again. He pushed me back until I was folded in half and he pistoned into me, fucking me as I had never been fucked before. His cock hit depths never yet explored, and I found myself crying as the pleasure was more than I could bear.

I stroked my cock quickly, knowing it wouldn't be long before I exploded. It ached; it was so fucking hard.

"Ollie... I'm so... fuck... that's' so... no ones ever fucked me like this.. before... I'm gonna... Ollie fuck... Kiss me..." I begged as he slowed his pace, and his breathing became rapid. He was about to cum too. His mouth found mine, and I mumbled as he kissed me. "Ollie, I love you..."

"I love you too," he said as I came all over my chest. He pulled out of me and stroked himself quickly and exploded in rivulets all over my stomach, soaking me in more cum than I had ever seen before. I fingered it and slowly popped it into my mouth, tasting him. He kissed me again, and I knew he could taste himself on my tongue.

"That was..."

"More than I could have ever imagined," I answered for him.

"I was going to say all right..." he chuckled. "You are... Sebastian?"

"I know..."

"Do you really have to go?" he said huskily.

"Just hold me, Oliver... We can talk about that in the morning."

I never slept better in my entire life as I did in his arms. How could I leave when I finally realized my heart was here?

19

Sebastian

I woke up the next morning, sticky as shit. Oliver was purring in his sleep, his thick muscular arm thrown over me. I gently and quietly unwound myself from his body, and he turned over and curled into a ball, still asleep. He looked like an angel.

So peaceful, so beautiful.

So, fucking manly.

Jesus.

I had to stifle my giggles when I saw his chest hair matted with our goo. We really should have showered last night, but both of us were so spent, all we could do was curl up and pass out together. Sex with Oliver was a fucking workout.

I thought I noticed a bathroom downstairs when I first entered, and I made my way back there, happily finding a shower. The hot water woke me up and invigorated me. The soap and shampoo smelled of sandalwood, and I washed last night's lovemaking off of my body. I dried off quickly and pulled my clothes back on, digging in my pocket for my cellphone.

I had to make a call. Now, before my courage failed me. I knew what it was I had to do, or I would regret it for the rest of my life.

I pulled up my agent and dialed his number.

"Seb, my boy! How's the wild west? You have no idea how many people are interested in you, right now. Hot my boy… You're steaming up the place here in the city. Why did I hear from an agent friend in LA that you are directing Blake Hudson? He's a star, Seb and now I am getting offers for you to direct TV. Seriously, you are hot as hell right now. What can I do for you, my boy?" I grinned at the knowledge my career was still on the rise. That was not going to make this easier, though.

"Jerry? Can you sublet my apartment for me? I mean, have an assistant help me with that. I am going to stay here for a while, maybe even move here permanently… I don't know… I mean…"

"What's his name?" Jerry said seriously. "Are you in love with this schmuck? Don't answer that… You're not a fool, Seb. Sure… You're not quitting on me, are you? I mean, the offers… Seb… You are gonna be so excited, but it doesn't really matter where you live, kid. As long as you make it in for the work, you can live wherever you damn well please."

"I think I am, Jerry… Thank you. When are you gonna tell me what my next show is?" I asked, hopefully, feeling like I could do this. I could have aunt Helen and Oliver and this fucking magical place. My heart was here in The Pleasant, and I wasn't sure I would ever want to leave. I mean… for work, of course. But this is where I would come back to. Oliver was who I would come back to.

Of course, I would have to tell him.

"I'll bring them in person, and we can decide when I see you. Are you kidding me, Seb? I've already booked a flight and a cabin to see what you do with Blake in Noises Off. Kid, you are on the brink of greatness. Trust me."

Funnily enough, I did.

20

Oliver

"Sebastian!" Helen called from downstairs. "Before you go, honey, can you bring down my copy of California Suite? It should be in the small bookcase in my office by the desk. I think!"

"Neil Simon? Really, Helen?" I called as I threw a tank top on. I walked into her office and found it easily. She was the most organized person in the world. Her collection of plays had always inspired me. Bookcases stood against the walls filled to the brim with scripts and scores. Helen took programming a season for the theatre very seriously.

I ran down the stairs taking them two at a time, just as I always did when I was younger. Old habits die hard, I guess. "Here you go. Are you really thinking of pulling that old play out for the fall?"

"No... I just wanted to read it." I handed it to her, and she laid it in her lap and beamed up at me, the happiest of smiles. "I can't believe you are staying, honey. I just want to say, once again, that I'm okay. You don't have to stay for me."

"I'm not, Helen. You are just the icing on top, I promise. I'm staying for myself. I want to see where this goes," I bent down and kissed her on her cheek. She reached up and ruffled my hair gently.

"No regrets?" She kissed me back.

"Life is too short, Helen. I won't be out too late, promise."

"Honey, you stay out as late as you want. Give Oliver my love."

I got in her car and realized I should probably get my own. I had never owned a car before, so that could be fun. Maybe I would get a truck. So butch...

I drove over to Oliver's, and he hopped in the car.

"So, where are we going?" I asked him.

"Really? I thought you would have figured it out by now," he groaned, giving me a playful and loving smile.

"Ahhh..." I nodded. "That makes sense."

I drove us to the beach, and I saw the bonfire roaring from the parking lot. Our gaggle of friends already there drinking and having fun.

Oliver took my hand and led me down the pathway that would take us to the festivities. Crystal's loud cackle traveled across the sandy beach to us, letting us know that they were in riotous spirits. Blake's deep voice boomed as he called out to Danny. We heard his voice answer further away. Must have had to use the bathroom or something.

Soon we saw him jog back towards the fire, his outline dark against the moon's glow.

"Slim and Ollie, finally!" Crystal screamed as she jumped up and ran over to us, giving each of us a quick hug. "Come on... We made hot dogs for some ungodly reason."

I laughed loudly. "I'm good."

"I'm hungry..." Oliver answered sweetly. God, I just wanted to kiss him.

We walked up to the bonfire, and everyone said hi. Blake scooted over and made room for us between himself and Sam.

"Sebastian, this is my almost-husband, Grayson." A tall slab of muscle and matinee idol looks stood up. Even in the red light of the fire, it was easy to see this man was handsome as fuck. Sam grinned widely, excited for me to meet him.

"I have heard a lot about you. So, do we call you Slim or Sebastian?" Grayson asked, shaking my hand.

"He's not so slim anymore," Danny whistled. "Slim worked out."

"He used to be so tall and skinny..." Crystal shrugged.

"How about you call me, Seb. I've gotten used to it over the years." I looked around at everyone, and they laughed happily.

"Seb it is," Hunter shouted loudly. He must be a little drunk. Kris reached over and kissed him on the cheek. It was so nice to see them together again.

"Well, here we all are, again. It's funny, isn't it? Those that leave, always return to The Pleasant." Evan said seriously. "The gang is almost all back together."

"Well..." Crystal sighed.

"I said almost..." Evan shrugged and laughed sadly. We all knew who he meant. No one had heard from him in years. When Tyler left, he left for good and burned all the bridges on the way out of town.

"Oliver?" I whispered in his ear.

He leaned back ad whispered into mine. "What, baby?"

"Did you hear the news, everyone?" Blake suddenly asked. "Seb, here," he put his hand on my shoulder and squeezed, "Is going to be directing me this winter in a TV movie. His agent just settled. I'm excited to work with you again. This summer was amazing."

"Yeah! That's awesome!" Kris smiled broadly, his head leaning on Hunter's broad shoulder.

"I know. My first time directing a film, ever. I'm fucking terrified. It's going to be a crazy fall, though. I'll be in San Diego for six weeks directing a musical that's trying to get to Broadway and then this film in November for five weeks. At least I'll have some time off to be back here." I snuggled closer to Oliver, who put his arm around my waist and pulled me in tightly.

"What were you gonna say?" Oliver whispered again.

"I've never been happier. I love you, Ollie," I answered.

He kissed me on the cheek and breathed the scent of me in deeply.

"Always."

I was in love and the night was beautiful.

I was back where I belonged, and the future was electric.

THE END

The Point Pleasant Books

THE POINT PLEASANT HOLIDAY SERIES (A Hallmark-(ish) Romance Series)

The Rites of Spring Break- (a second chance romance)
Second chance at love!

The Point Pleasant Books

Spring Break Shenanigans!
And a very hot firefighter!
mybook.to/SecondChanceRomance

Something Borrowed Something Boo (Fall wedding/Hollywood star in small town)

Halloween? Check.
Halloween Wedding? Double check.
Falling in love unexpectedly at the Halloween wedding?
Totally Inconvenient!
mybook.to/gayhallmarkish

A Very Merry Princemas (Hidden Prince at Christmas)

The Point Pleasant Books

A hidden Prince in a small town.
An event planner overwhelmed with the Christmas Ball.
Will love overcome? Most definitely!
mybook.to/Princemas

Cupid, Draw Back Your Beau (Age-Gap Valentine)

The Point Pleasant Books

A young man wishing for love.
A single dad hoping to love again.
A wild round of Speed dating! It must be Valentines day!
mybook.to/ValentinesGay

Hart Belongs To Daddy (Rockstar Age-gap romance)

The Point Pleasant Books

A Rockstar post nervous breakdown
A young man recovering from loss
All the gay Hallmark-(ish) feels you crave as they save the town bookstore from corporate takeover

mybook.to/HartBelongsToDaddy

About Shane K Morton

Shane lives in Studio city with his husband and their fur baby, Slayer. His novels include: The Trouble With Off-Campus Housing, Private Waterloos, The Year of the Cock, Fault Lines and The Point Pleasant Holiday Series. His Dark Romance books, written under Sean Azinsalt, include: It's in My Blood as well as Dark Eros. When not writing, Shane can usually be found at a film festival or performing cabaret in a dark dive bar.

Join Shane's Facebook Group- Sweet And Salty
Follow him on Bookbub- https://www.bookbub.com/profile/shane-k-morton
Join the **mailing list** and get access to a **FREE** short story in the Point Pleasant World- https://claims.prolificworks.com/free/0Xa3gZvB

Made in United States
North Haven, CT
09 February 2026